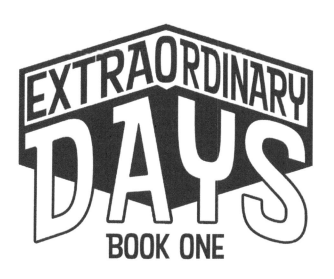

BOOK ONE

BY
ROBERT RAY SEEGER

Dedication

To my amazing children, beautiful wife, and the adventures we have together. May we have many more. Oh. And I guess to the dumb dog too.

CHAPTER

01

HAPPILY EVER BEFORE

Life for the Seeger children was full of laughter. Few days had ever been bad, and almost none had ever been difficult. To be honest, Edith, Wilber, and Ana had never known a day of sorrow. Yes, they had been sad, and yes, they had experienced pain, but they had never been heartbroken.

They spent their summers in the shade of an ash tree in their backyard. Days were filled with swimming pools, swing sets, and sandboxes. At night, they caught fireflies and roasted marshmallows in the firepit. During winter, they sat together on the couch, drank hot cocoa, and watched the snow fall. Christmas was spent with cousins and caroling around the basement piano.

But this family was not defined by what they did. They were instead defined by what they believed. It was a household built on God, and all blessings flowed from that.

Edith was the oldest at 7. Although she was good at many things, she was mostly known for her heart. She cared deeply for people, and she went out of her way to make everyone feel loved. There was no sweeter girl in the whole world. She hid her sensitive heart behind a shy smile and a gentle touch.

Her brother Wilber was 5, and he was known for much. He was the loudest, the stinkiest, and the most dangerous. When you weren't looking, he was the one most likely to jump on your back and tackle you to the ground. He was most likely to giggle at the wrong time and burp after he was told to be quiet. Even though he was most likely to hurt himself or someone else, he was also the source of much laughter.

Ana was the youngest at 2. She had big eyes and chubby cheeks. Although completely capable of walking, she usually chose not to. Instead, her curly blonde head would dive into the nearest person for hugs and cuddles. She was fierce and rebellious, often putting her parents in challenging situations.

Life was good... but that was about to change. Extraordinary days were coming. The days ahead would be filled with awe and wonder, but they would also be filled with hardships and pain. Life does this from time to time. It takes twists and turns and throws you up and down, but God always has his reasons. Mysterious are his plans. So while some people get a "happily ever after," the Seeger kids lived their "happily ever before."

On the day everything changed, Edith got up early. She helped Dada make French toast and set the table. Ana lay in her crib, cooing to the tune of "Jesus Loves Me." Wilber crawled under the table and played video games. The family dog, Rebel, lay beside him, waiting patiently for food to fall on the floor.

"Wilber," Mama said, pulling him out by his ankle. "No more screens."

"Yes, Mama," he said, still playing the game as Mama dragged him across the kitchen floor.

Dada carried a plate across the kitchen and sat it down on the table. "Breakfast is ready."

Edith sat down on the bench by the big window. "What are we going to do today?"

Mama was beside her. "We have church today," she said, trying to keep Ana from slapping her with a spoon.

"Oh, right," Edith nodded.

Dada grabbed a white jar from Wilber. "That's enough powdered sugar," Dada said, setting the container on the other side of the table.

Already, Wilber's small piece of toast was covered in a mountain of white powder. He greedily examined the meal with wide eyes. "Just right," he whispered to himself.

"How about after?" Edith asked.

"I don't know," Mama said, turning to Ana. "Oh, sweet girl, what have you done?"

Curls of blonde hair remained frozen above her head like antlers. Syrup was everywhere, dripping from the baby fork that had somehow gotten stuck in her bangs. There was even a strip of bacon tangled somewhere in back. Every time Mama reached for the fork, Ana slapped her hand.

"No. No," Ana said, mimicking Mama's *I'm Angry* tone. She crossed her arms, glaring at her mother. It was a warning, one the baby gave often. Sometimes it was meant to be sassy, other times, rude, but it always meant Ana was not happy. This particular time, the growling tone told the family something big: Ana was about to lose her flipping mind.

This was always a delicate dance for the parents. They knew Ana was just a baby, but they also knew God didn't want them—as Dada often said—raising deadbeats or dictators. The parents took this calling seriously. Mama put her hands on her hips and looked menacingly at her daughter. Dada stood beside her. Wilber and Edith held their breath.

All eyes were on Ana... and that's why no one saw Rebel creeping towards the kitchen. In a flash, the puppy was on the table. It had been a setup! Ana and the dog had planned the whole thing. Ana clapped happily as the puppy ate the food, a couple forks, and a butter dish.

"Go, Rebi," she cheered as the dog dodged out of Mama's reach. This caused a gallon of milk to fall off the table and onto Dada's lap.

"Darn it, Rebel," Dada yelled at the dog. "Go outside!"

But Rebel wouldn't. He wouldn't go anywhere... not until he was captured or had a belly full of people-food. The puppy rarely got treats like this. In fact, Ana was the only one that helped Rebel get forbidden snacks like gummy bears, dead birds, cake, and toilet water.

In the puppy's tiny brain, he never imagined getting anything as good as this. A whole breakfast, all to himself, and he wasn't going to waste it. He moved fast, but when he saw Wilber's plate of powdered sugar, he doubled in speed.

Rebel lunged for it, but the powdered sugar from Wilber's plate made the dog sneeze. A blast of steamy dog breath shot from the puppy's nose, covering Wilber with powdered sugar boogers.

"Disgusting," Edith said, holding her plate as a shield.

Dada reached for Rebel, finally grabbing him by the collar. "That's it," he said, dragging the dog off the table and outside. He shut the door and walked back into the kitchen.

No one said anything for a few seconds. They just sat there, stunned. Breakfast was ruined.

Wilber wiped green goo and white powder from his eyes. Edith pulled chunks of eggs from her hair, and Ana gave Rebel a thumbs-up through the window.

Dada turned to Mama, "Well, My Love, do you want to clean the kitchen or the baby?"

A rumble roared from deep within Ana's stomach. It

grew louder as it exited her body and shook the highchair. "Poo-poo," she giggled.

"I'll clean the kitchen," Mama said, sliding the highchair over to Dada as Ana let out a second thunder toot. "Yes, definitely the kitchen."

After the children had baths, they played on the back deck.

Ana was sitting under the grill next to the propane tank. She had one end of a stick in her mouth, and Rebel had the other in his jaws. The two gnawed on it furiously, each growling when one pulled too hard.

Wilber sat in a lawn chair with his bare feet on a log. He found the hunk of wood and kept it because it resembled a camel. But not just any camel. It looked exactly like the one who spit on him at the Lincoln Zoo. He later told the elderly woman across the street that it was the best thing that ever happened to him. Much to his disappointment, Mama washed the shirt, erasing the spit stain and ruining his most prized possession.

"Want to play a game?" Wilber asked his sisters.

Next to him were his rain boots. He was careful to put each on the wrong foot. It hadn't rained for weeks, nor was it going to. He just liked the sound they made when he stomped through the house (and he liked Mama's angry reaction even more).

Edith was playing with her favorite doll, Grapey. It was a garage sale purchase named after the purple pants she came with. It was an ordinary toy, except for the bandage over her right wrist. No one was sure who chewed off the doll's hand, Ana or Rebel, but Edith took the injury surprisingly well. While most girls her age would have pouted or even cried, Edith sprung into action. She rushed to the medicine cabinet, grabbed a few things, and nurtured the doll back to good health.

"You can play house with me and Grapey," Edith said, brushing the doll's hair. She then sang Mama's favorite lullaby, rocking the baby to sleep. The tune had a similar effect on Ana. The baby took the stick out of her mouth, and her eyes began to droop.

"That sounds bo-ring," Wilber said, punting a basketball off the deck.

"I can't wait until church," Edith said, putting the doll down in a chair as if it were a crib. "I miss our friends."

Wilber pointed to the sky. "What in the world is that?"

At first, it was nothing more than a pink speck, but

they could hear a terrible noise as it grew closer. It sounded like a shoe in the washing machine. The banging got louder and louder until the children could finally see it clearly. High above the clouds, a pink and shimmering ship was falling from space.

Ana and Rebel both covered their ears and hid behind the grill, whining loudly.

"Is it going to crash on us?" Wilber asked, screaming to be heard over the noise.

"Watch out!" Edith grabbed Wilber's hand and pulled him under the patio table.

The object was almost on top of them when it dropped out of view in the neighbor's yard. While it didn't hit with much force, it did shake everything around them. Squirrels fell out of trees, and the baby pool bounced onto the roof.

Wilber was the first one to crawl out of hiding. He slowly peeked his head out from under the table. "Look, Edith."

On the other side of the fence, there was a massive cloud of bubbles and white smoke. They rose to the sky and filled the air with a salty-smelling breeze. As the smoke dissipated, a gigantic wave of water gushed through the fence slats and flooded the yard.

Edith shivered. "What do you think it is?" she asked.

"Let's go see," Wilber said, running across the deck. Rebel followed him.

Edith picked Ana up and cautiously followed her brother. "I don't think this is a good idea."

Wilber ran down the deck stairs and jumped over the last three steps. "Come on, Edith. It's gonna be... AWESOME!"

Edith was careful to take each step as she carried Ana to the yard. "You don't know that," she said, sounding like Mama. "It's probably dangerous."

"That's actually true. I fink it might be dangerous... but it might also be awesome!"

Wilber climbed the fence easily. Edith and Ana watched Rebel lap up water flowing into the yard.

Wilber's eyes opened wide. "It's a giant seashell," he said, both puzzled and amazed.

CHAPTER

02
MAGIC WINDOW

Edith and Ana looked through the slats on the fence. Through them, they could see a giant conch shell. It was as big as the shed. Sunlight hit the smooth surface, and pink rays shimmered in the morning light. Water spilled from fresh cracks and flowed from inside. It squirted out and onto the ground, flooding the grass, reminding them of the time Wilber forgot to turn off the hose.

Edith held her breath. "Listen," she said.

A small voice came from inside the shell. "Help!"

"Someone needs us," Edith said.

Wilber jumped off the fence. He landed on the wet grass, and water splashed all over the girls.

"Hey!" Edith yelled, trying to shield Ana.

"We should help," he said, heading for the gate.

Edith held him back. "Are you sure?" she asked. "It might be too dangerous for Ana."

The baby frowned and slapped Edith on the top of her head. "No. No," Ana said sternly.

Edith frowned. "You two always get me in trouble." She stomped her foot, again splashing water everywhere.

Ana giggled and clapped her chubby hands on Edith's face. She kissed her sister on the nose and said, "Moof."

At the same time, the voice from inside the shell cried again. "Please," she begged. "Help me."

"Alright," Edith said, giving in.

Both Wilber and Rebel nodded with big open-mouth smiles. The children ran to the side gate, went through the pine trees, and into the yard with the shell. By the time they got to the massive conch, water had finally stopped flowing from within. The voice had also grown faint. "Help," she said, choking on the word.

The water had pooled in the low parts of the yard,

and it was up to their ankles. Edith's shoes and socks were soaked, but Wilber's obsession with rain boots was finally paying off. Ana, on the other hand, waited at the water's edge. "Ughhhhh," she said, pointing at the water. Edith walked back across the puddle to pick her up. Wilber led them through the sloshy grass.

They walked around the giant seashell until they found the opening. Inside, there was a large iron door. It was covered with barnacles and rust. A giant dent spread from the top of the door to the bottom.

Edith pointed to a small crack. "That must be how the water got out."

Wilber grabbed the handle. "Help me open it."

The door screeched as they pushed against it. Inside, the children found a little room. Seaweed covered everything. It smelled like their vacation to Galveston, and it reminded them of the cousins who went with them. Seafoam covered the walls, but some of the bubbles were as large as windows. Inside these orbs, the children could see images. Most of them showed the view outside the shell, just as if they were windows. Others showed something... *else.*

Edith stepped closer and gazed inside. "Is this a movie or real life?"

"I fink real," Wilber said, examining the images closely. "They don't look like a movie or video game to me."

Through bubbles, they watched a war being waged in the sky above Jupiter. Shells flew through space, swooping as they shot tridents at a much larger ship. Their enemy, while greater in size, was trashed. That's not to say it was not older or more run down; it was like an actual dump glued together and sent into space. By comparison, the seashells looked like fairies swarming a pile of garbage. However, the dump ship had powerful lasers. With every shot, the shell ships were quickly destroyed.

Edith set Ana on the ground and touched the bubble's glassy surface. "They're like magic computer screens," Edith said.

"I fink the trash pile is winning," Wilber added.

Ana squealed, "Fishy!"

Her brother and sister turned to the baby. A mermaid lay crumpled on the ground in front of her. Her hair was long and blonde, braided together with nets, fishing lines, and strings of pearls. Green scales covered her tail, and her fins were as soft as silk.

Edith bent down and held the mermaid's hand. "Are

you okay?"

She was gasping, struggling to breathe. Her gills were shriveled and dry. "We came... because... there are spies," she said, coughing. "The orcs of Babylon... are already here... and your planet... is in danger." Speaking took a lot out of the mermaid, making her peach skin grow pale and her scales grey.

"She's dying," Wilber screamed. "What do we do?"

There was still a little bit of water left in the shell. It pooled on the floor, so Ana splashed as much as possible onto the mermaid. That seemed to bring life and color back to her body.

"Good job, Ana," shouted Wilber. "But I fink she's going to need a lot more."

"The orcs... already destroyed... my world," she choked. "Yours... is next."

Edith's eyes grew wide. "What do we do?"

"Take... my ring," she said, gasping.

Edith and Wilber froze.

"Moof!" Ana shouted. She pulled the ring off the mermaid's finger and popped it in her mouth. With Rebel leading the way, she crawled out of the ship on her hands and knees.

"Wait for us, Ana!" Wilber put one of the mermaid's

arms around his shoulders. "Edith, help me."

Edith grabbed her other arm, and they carried her out of the shell. Her beautiful tail drug on the ground as they dragged her through the neighbor's yard.

Ana was already at the fence. She turned around and smiled at her siblings. With an open mouth, she yelled again. "Moof." Light shot from the ring and out of her mouth as if it had a life of its own. It pointed for them to go forward.

Wilber laughed. "Ana's like a little baby flashlight!"

Edith nodded in agreement.

"Wait," the mermaid gasped. She lifted a small barnacle-covered device and pointed it at the ship. The whole thing immediately shrunk down to the size of a standard conch shell. It fell to the ground and splashed in the grass. She tried to reach for it, but her arms fell limp.

"What in the name of the law?" Wilber asked.

"Don't worry. I'll get it," Edith said, leaning down to pick it up.

"Go. Go. Go," Ana repeated. With each movement of her lips, light escaped her mouth. "Moof now."

"Hurry," the mermaid urged. Her head wobbled on her shoulders, and her eyes sagged.

The ring in Ana's mouth led them to a cluster of pine trees in the neighbor's yard. They followed the light inside until it pointed to a pinecone on the ground.

"What should we do?" Edith asked.

"Hurry," the mermaid said. "Open… it."

Wilber frowned. "I fink she's crazy!"

"Here," Edith said, letting go of the mermaid. She walked over to the pinecone and picked it up. Instead of coming up easy, this pinecone was heavy. A large chunk of the ground came up with it, pivoting like a hinge. The pinecone was like a doorknob, and on the other side, there was a whirlpool of pine needles and light. Through the swirling flashes of blinding light, they saw something that looked like a city.

"Should we go in?" Wilber exclaimed.

"Babylon… is here… will kill… us all," the mermaid said. Her voice wavered, and she then passed out.

Edith put her hands on her cheeks. "I think we should ask Mama and Dada for help."

Wilber nodded, but Ana jumped right in before they could stop her. She splashed through the portal and disappeared.

"Ana, no!" Edith screamed, but it was already too late. "Now what?"

Wilber shoved the mermaid into the portal. Her head went in first, and then her tail slid completely inside the magic window. "You know what Dada always says. We gotta protect each other."

Edith thought for a second and eventually grabbed Wilber's hand. "Alright. On the count of three?"

Wilber nodded.

"One... two..." she said as Rebel jumped in.

Wilber screamed, "THREE!" and they jumped in. As they did, the pinecone door fell shut, leaving no evidence of anything extraordinary. Only a soppy wet yard.

CHAPTER

03

FAR OUT ISLAND

Wilber and Edith fell from a hole in the sky and landed violently on a hard metal surface. Edith banged her elbow, and Wilber twisted his ankle. Both children tried to get up, but their heads felt wobbly and their bodies weak.

"Ugh," Wilber said. "I fink I'm going to frow up."

Edith rolled onto her back. "I'm not feeling the best either." The cold metal felt good on her skin.

As the dizziness wore off, they slowly became more aware of their surroundings. For the first time, they could hear Ana. She cried loudly next to the mermaid.

Wilber rolled onto his hands and knees. "Mermaid, you doin okay?"

There was no response.

Rebel was chewing on the mermaid's tail.

"No, Rebel," Edith said. She smacked him on the side. "She's a person. Not food."

Rebel hung his head in shame, and his big puppy eyes grew teary.

Wilber looked around. "Where are we?"

The children found themselves on a large metal stage. It was the size of their private school's football field, but instead of having bleachers and a concession stand, this one hung off the side of a cliff. It hovered over a terrifyingly dark chasm, and they couldn't see the bottom.

"Look over there," Wilber said, pointing to a tall structure. Beautiful shades of red and purple adorned the surface, but it was also covered with terrible-looking spikes. "Is that a tower?"

"There's another one over there," Edith said. "I've never seen anything like that in Lincoln."

The towers weren't connected to the stage. Instead, they disappeared into the chasm. A giant orb sat on the top of each tower, and they were white and glassy.

"Are they lighthouses?" Edith asked.

Wilber shrugged. "There's no light."

Behind them was an island. They could see forests, a lake, a few mountains, and rivers from where they stood, but there was also a city. Small buildings populated much of the surface. While most were the size of homes, shops, and other small businesses, a few were the size of skyscrapers. The island was also filled with other mysterious objects, one of which was a giant sword. Its blade stuck into the ground, and it rose taller than the buildings.

And if that wasn't incredible enough, the view in front of them was breathtaking. Like an ocean, they stood before space... outer space. There were planets, asteroids, black holes, and a million galaxies.

Wilber murmured to himself. "Where did that portal take us?"

"It's incredible," Edith said.

As she spoke, the two stiff towers twisted and bent inward. They stretched and grew as they arched to where the children stood. At the center of each glassy white orb, there were big black dots. They spun and focused until each one pointed at the children.

Edith took a step back, her mouth agape. "Are

those... eyes?"

And they were. Eyes. Two giant ones. Each one was planted firmly on what the children thought were towers. They bent and moved like the antenna of some giant insect. With great intentionality, the pupils focused on the children: first on Edith, then Wilber, Ana, and lastly, Rebel. After a few seconds of strict examination, the giant eyes turned to the mermaid. When the eyes focused on her, the pupils doubled in size.

"Trespassers," boomed a loud voice. The sound came from the darkness underneath the stage. The slight vibrations tickled their feet, and the feeling rose to their bellies.

Ana giggled.

"We're not dress pastors," Wilber said, frowning. "Not very, we are."

The voice boomed again. "Well, I don't know who you are, and only approved people can use rings. Otherwise, no one is allowed on my island."

"I'm Edith. This is my brother Wilber, and that's my baby sister, Ana. This is our pet labrador, Rebel." After introducing her family, Edith turned and pointed to the mermaid. "But we don't know who she is."

Wilber spoke in a voice that made him sound far more confident than he felt. "She crashed her seashell into our neighbor's backyard," he explained. "She asked us for help."

"Her name is Sushi," the voice boomed, sending the vibrations through the air a second time. Ana giggled again.

Edith clapped her hands. "Oh good, you know her."

"I told you," the voice exploded. "I know everyone on my island. I've called, and help should be arriving shortly."

"You'd need a hundred infinity billion dollars to buy an island," Wilber said, rolling his eyes. "I doubt you have that much money, so how can it be your island?" As he spoke, he turned back to the island city and the endless space that surrounded it.

"Because it's on *my* back," the voice said.

Now, when the children looked around, they saw something completely different. Yes, they were on a large metal stage, and yes, there was an island behind them. But what they hadn't seen—not until that moment—was this: everything they saw had grown on the back of a giant crab.

"Amazing," Edith said.

Under the island was a massive hard-shelled body, not to mention ten huge legs. They were impossibly long and stretched out across space. Each leg perched on a different asteroid, and the whole thing rested like a spider on a web of stars.

The children stood on the edge, trying to glimpse the ginormous creature. They peered into the darkness below and marveled. As they did, a giant claw rose to the sky in front of them. It was purple and red, just like the color surrounding the eyes. The pinchers were big enough to cut a building or club a mountain to pieces. With all the grace of a princess, it waved at them.

"What are you?" Wilber asked.

"I'm Uncle Ned," the voice boomed. "What else would I be?"

Ana waved. "Huhwoh."

But Uncle Ned was distracted. His big black pupils were pointed back at the city. "Ah. Finally," he said. "Here comes Captain Jimmy Rustbeard. He'll help."

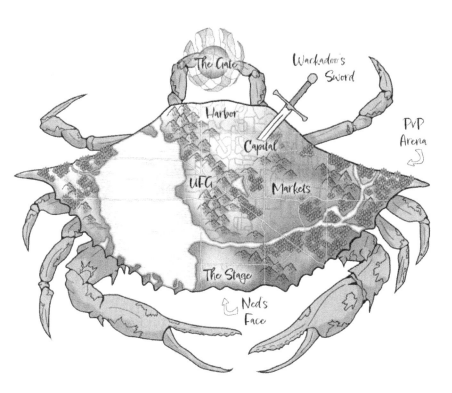

Map of Uncle Ned

CHAPTER

04

JIMMY RUSTBEARD

The children turned back to the island.

A small star and a dozen smaller moons orbited Uncle Ned, and they were just rising on his left side. In the distance, there was a small fishing village. Docks stretched off the shore and hovered in the nothingness of space. They floated weightlessly as if in water. Flying boats and dragons loaded and unloaded cargo as the light shone upon them.

Between them and the village, a small path stretched down through a wheat field. A tall metallic figure was running on long skinny legs along the trail.

Even from a distance, his reflective body shimmered in the starlight.

"Ahoy," Rustbeard hollered.

Upon closer inspection, the children could see he was a robot with a shiny gold body. His long legs wiggled and stretched weirdly as he ran. There was a speaker for his mouth and two light bulbs for eyes. A bright green parrot sat nestled in his rust-colored beard.

Edith pointed to the sleeping mermaid. "Can you help her?" she asked.

"Yar," he said, stopping where Sushi lay. "The name's Captain Jimmy Rustbeard. This here be my parrot. I call her Tickles."

In response, the bird cawed. "Tickles wants loot," she screeched.

Wilber winced, looking at the bird, annoyed.

"Now, let me see," Rustbeard said. His voice crackled as he spoke—as if his speaker was not tuned to the right radio station. He knelt next to the mermaid and examined her closely. His left eye-bulb lit up and painted the mermaid's body with white light.

"Outta the water too long, I reckon," he explained. "She'll be needing more than I can give."

"Don't give up," Edith begged. "Please do something for her."

Wilber nodded in agreement.

Rustbeard pulled out a tiny jug from his pouch, took out the cork, and sniffed it.

"What's that?" Wilber asked.

"This here be the last of my healing tonic."

"Where'd you find that?" Wilber asked. He eyed the dirty jar, scrunching his face as if eating something sour.

"It be loot I found deep inside a giant shark," he explained, pouring the contents onto the mermaid. "Not made for her kind, but it'll help."

The liquid fell on the mermaid. She breathed the liquid into her gills, and although she eventually gasped, she never opened her eyes.

Wilber raised an eyebrow. "You went inside a shark?"

"Of course," the pirate said, his voice again crackling. "Where else I be getting a healing tonic?"

Wilber shrugged. "I don't know. The store?"

"Tickles," Rustbeard said to the bird in his beard. "Alert the Medbay. I'll carry her to the nearest depot, but the medics need to have a salt bath ready."

"Salt bath for Tickles," the parrot said with a happy

crow. She hopped out of the robot's beard and swooped happily above them.

"Nay, ye foolish bird." Rustbeard swatted at the bird with his pirate hat. "For Sushi. Salt bath FOR SUSHI."

"Caw!" the parrot crowed, flying back to town. "Salt bath for Sushi and Tickles. Caw!"

Rustbeard shook his head and put his hat back on his head. "I'd cook and eat that dumb bird... or I would if I ever ate anything besides batteries," he mumbled, lifting Sushi in his big, long arms.

"Will she be okay?" Edith asked. "We've been so worried."

"Arg, don't lose heart," his voice said with static. "She'll be fine, but only because of you. Ye saved her life."

"Yay-hoo," Wilber said, fist-pumping the air.

Edith picked up Ana, and the two girls laughed. "We did it, Ana," Edith said in a baby voice. Rebel barked as Wilber patted his head.

"Well done," Uncle Ned said, shaking the stage with a happy booming tone. "Usually, humans are so worthless."

Now that the mermaid was safe, the children were fully aware of their situation. They were deep in outer space, far from home, and on the back of the giant crab. The children looked at each other. Each could see they all felt the same thing.

"Mama," Ana said, tears forming in her eyes.

"Yeah," Wilber agreed. "I wanna go home too."

Edith set Ana down on the stage. "Uncle Ned," Edith said. "Do you know how we can get home?"

The two glass orbs turned back to the children. "Depends on where you want to go. I can probably take you home since rings only go one way," Uncle Ned explained. "Where is your home?"

"Lincoln, Nebraska," Edith said.

Uncle Ned didn't say anything for a while. He just stared, so Wilber added, "It's on Earth."

"Which one?" asked Uncle Ned.

Wilber shrugged, so Uncle Ned's eyes turned from the children to space. Each eye swiveled and looked around, moving independently from the other. The eyes moved and looked all over before he finally spoke.

"Ah," he said. "There it is. I'll have to travel through a few dimensions and go back in time to get there, but it won't be much work for me. Hold on."

One of Uncle Ned's large claws reached up and cut through space. It was like a sheet hung in front of them, hiding another reality behind it.

With great speed, Uncle Ned took off. The crab jumped and darted in. He skipped over stars and jumped from planet to planet before tearing open another hole in space. Again, he crept in and continued his journey through the stars.

"'There's an infinite number of worlds, and each one has its own story," he explained. "Some are covered in oceans, like Sushi's homeworld. Some are populated with dinosaurs, others with kings and queens, some with Chupacabra and bigfoot."

"What about unicorns," Edith asked, excited. "Is there a world full of unicorns?"

"Loads. We just passed one."

"What about video games?" Wilber asked.

"More than you can count," Uncle Ned said with a chuckle. "But worlds can also be important for what they do, not just who lives there. Some are for fighting famous wars, reliving beloved eras of history, or centered on scientific advancements like steam-power or computers."

Planets whizzed by and changed as Uncle Ned took them farther into the past. Some had big cities that shrunk until they were just small towns. Others had spaceships that rewound all the way back to horse-drawn carriages.

"All of this looks like so much fun," Edith said, watching a planet of leprechauns go from having jetpacks to baking cookies in a treehouse.

"But some of these worlds are sad," Uncle Ned warned. "They were destroyed for one reason or another: nuclear wars, zombies, tornadoes, evil rulers— you know, nightmare stuff. There are a million reasons a world can go sad, but most go sad because of Babylon."

Suddenly, Wilber remembered what Sushi had said. "What is Babylon?" he asked.

Edith nodded. "Sushi said they might be coming to Earth. That we had spies or something."

Uncle Ned slowed to a stop. The stars stopped moving, and the crab barely inched forward. He said nothing.

Edith was hesitant. "Uncle Ned, what's wrong?"

"If Babylon put spies on your homeworld, then it is done for," Uncle Ned explained, his voice soft for the first time. There was a slight tremble when he spoke. "I'm the only world in history to survive an invasion from Babylon. But look what it cost me."

Uncle Ned pointed to the giant sword stabbed into

his back. They were miles from the blade, yet they could still see the thing high above the horizon.

"The people on my back only survived because I could run," Uncle Ned explained. "Can your world run?"

The kids looked at each other. They eventually shook their head.

"No," Wilber admitted. "I fink it spins or something." He moved his hands around, trying to show everyone his understanding of the solar system. The faster he moved his hands, the more Wilber realized he didn't know what he was doing, and the boy started to laugh.

"Maybe you could go somewhere else," the crab encouraged. "You could stay here. On my back. It's just a matter of time before your world dies."

Edith felt hot, angry tears forming in her eyes. "I want to go home."

"Yeah," Wilber agreed. "We want to see our parents."

"Mama," Ana chimed in.

Now, both of Uncle Ned's eyes focused on the children. "I know you do, but Babylon is unbeatable. I've seen what they do to other worlds, and it's not pretty."

Edith motioned to her siblings. "Uncle Ned, it's our

home. We can't just give up."

Uncle Ned lifted a claw to the sky. He opened a dozen portals, each showing the children a different world. People were crying, buildings were destroyed, and everything looked terrible. People were locked in cages while others were forced to work hard. "These are the worlds Babylon took over. And that was just this morning alone."

Edith imagined her house, school, and church being burned down. She imagined her friends and family in prison. Tears formed in her eyes, and her hands started shaking. She looked at her siblings and saw the same fear in their eyes.

"We won't let that happen," Wilber said. "We'll stop them."

"It's never happened," Uncle Ned said, showing them one more world filled with scary monsters. "This is Sushi's world, Mermoni. It used to be filled with beautiful castles and other marvelous things. Now it's just a place for spooky creatures to do bad things."

The children watched disgusting creatures capture merfolk and put them in nets. They even saw some mermaids and mermen die.

"Can't you help them?" Wilber asked.

Uncle Ned growled. "You're not listening. The only thing you can do is run or hide. That's the only way."

As fear rose in the hearts of all three children, so did something else. There was an unspoken bond of love between them, and it gave them courage.

"Thanks for offering," Edith said, standing tall and confident. "But we want to be with our parents."

"Yeah," Wilber agreed, wiping tears from his eyes. "If Babylon is coming for Earth, we will fight them together. And we're going to kick their big fat booties."

"Are you sure I can't talk you out of it?"

"No, Uncle Ned," Wilber said. "Take us home."

"Yesh," Ana agreed. Rebel barked.

The crab nodded by lowering his eyes. The whole world rose up and down with his movements. He jumped from universe to universe and world to world until they finally saw home. Earth was large in front of them, but it was still impossibly far away.

"If I get any closer, someone will see me," he explained. "But we are close enough. You'll have to jump."

Wilber pointed at the planet. "We can't jump!" he screamed. "It's still a million infinities away."

"Not off the stage," the giant crab explained. "I have

a special portal for short distances. Here."

A portal opened on the stage. It stretched out like a tunnel, and the children could see their backyard on the other side.

Mama was on the deck, looking over the railing. "Where are you guys?" she asked. "It's time to go."

Edith looked at Wilber, a little hesitant.

"Don't worry, gurl," he said with a smile. "I'll go first."

Wilber took a deep breath and dove into the floating portal. Although the tunnel stretched from the moon to earth, it felt more like a slide. After a few seconds, Wilber was through the tunnel and falling onto the grass. He stood up and dusted himself off. "It's safe!" he yelled through the tunnel.

Rebel jumped in and arrived safely on the other side.

"I guess we're next," Edith said. She took a deep breath and jumped with Ana in her arms.

CHAPTER

05

CAR RIDE CONFESSION

"Does everyone have everything?" Mama asked as the family loaded into the minivan. "Are we forgetting anything?"

As Edith crawled to the back, Wilber followed. She whispered to her brother, "Should we tell Mama and Dada what happened?"

Wilber nodded. "They won't either be mad."

"Even," Edith corrected. "Won't even be mad."

Mama buckled Ana while they crawled into their car seats. Edith examined Ana's face. She was just as worried... either that, or she had gas.

After everyone was buckled, Mama got in the passenger seat. Dada backed up the van and pulled out of the driveway. "Here we go," he said.

Wilber peeked around the chair. "Ana, what do you fink we should do?"

Ana pulled her pacifier out of her mouth. "Mrrrr arrrr," she said as if rolling a marble around in her mouth. Drool dribbled down her chin and onto her shirt.

"Gross," Wilber said with a giggle. "You're so distgusting."

Edith leaned closer. "What if they don't believe us? What if they are mad?"

Wilber fiddled with his seatbelt. "They say it's okay to tell them anything."

They both looked at each other, not sure what to do. Eventually, Edith took a deep breath. "Dada, what's the craziest thing you've ever seen?"

"Hmmm," Dada said, pulling the van out of the neighborhood. "One time, I picked up Wilber, and he licked my eyeball. He was Ana's age."

Wilber burst out laughing.

Edith stuck out her tongue. "Gross. You mean, he licked your eyelid?"

"No. My eyes were wide open. I saw the whole

thing," Dada explained. "That was pretty crazy."

"Dada, be serious," Edith said, folding her arms.

"I am serious. Lucky I didn't go blind."

Wilber leaned to the center aisle. "Dada," he asked, "what's Babylon?".

Dada looked up from the road and examined Wilber's reflection in the mirror. "What do you mean, bud? From the Bible?"

The van bounced down the road. It was a lovely spring day, and people were enjoying the outdoors. Wilber watched them walk their dogs and ride their bikes. He held up his hands. "I don't know."

"Well, Babylon could mean a couple things," he explained. "Do you remember Daniel?"

"Are you talking about Mrs. Mitchell's cat?" he asked.

"No. I mean from the Bible," Dada laughed.

It was easier to remember the cat. Daniel scratched Wilber's face last summer when he tried to put the angry feline on a remote-controlled car. "Not really," he eventually admitted.

"Well, Babylon wanted everyone to worship fake gods."

"Oh yeah," Wilber said, nodding. "They tried to feed

him to lions. For praying to God. But God saved him."

"Oh, oh, oh," Edith said excitedly. She tended to have a better memory when it came to Bible and school. Her mind flooded with random facts. "Babylon threw Shadrach, Meshach, and Abednego in the fire because they wouldn't betray God. And God saved them too."

"Good memory," Mama cheered, smiling from the front seat.

The van stopped at a red light, and the children looked out the window. Wilber scratched his head. "Is Babylon still alive today?"

"Not like it was," Dada said. "Later in the Bible, if a nation becomes evil and turns from God, they are called Babylon."

Edith thought carefully. "What does 'turn from God' mean?"

This time, Mama answered. "If kings and presidents hurt poor people, start a lot of wars, or trick their people... they're called Babylon."

"Oh." Wilber nodded. "So they're the bad guys."

Dada nodded while making a right turn. "Yeah, bud. They're the bad guys."

"But we don't have to be afraid of Babylon, right?" Wilber clarified.

"Eh," Dada said, shrugging his shoulders. "Most nations usually become like Babylon before they fall. It's in our nature. When humans get power, we usually become greedy and boss everyone around. Leaders usually end up hurting people to get what they want... even the people they are supposed to protect."

Wilber sighed. "That's what I was afraid of."

Edith's voice wavered. "Should we be scared?" she asked. "Of Babylon, I mean. If they were spying on us, would you be afraid?"

Mama turned to the children. "Why are you asking all these weird questions?"

Edith couldn't keep her bottom lip from quivering. "Someone told us Babylon was spying on our planet, and they were coming to take us over. And I'm scared."

Another light turned red, the van stopped, and Mama and Dada looked at each other.

"Alright, guys. What's going on?"

Reluctantly, the kids told their parents everything that had happened that morning. They talked about Sushi, Uncle Ned, and Babylon. After the children finished telling their stories, they waited. They expected Mama and Dada to be mad or not believe them, but the parents didn't say anything. Dada kept driving, and

Mama kept her eyes on the road.

The children watched as their parents whispered to each other.

Eventually, Dada spoke. "Well, that explains why you guys are acting so... crabby!" he said. No one laughed but him.

"Dada, we're not joking," Edith moaned.

"Yeah, we're serious," Wilber added.

"I'm sorry, guys. It's just that, with all this talk about mermaids, your story sounds... fishy!"

"Dada!" the children screamed, both at the same time.

Ana was stern. "No. No, Dada," she added.

"Seriously, Dada," Mama said, also annoyed. "Why can't you take anything seriously. You know what they're talking about."

The parents looked at each other, and although neither were talking, the children could see they were communicating. Dada eventually nodded before speaking again.

Mama turned to the children at the back of the van. She looked each of them in the eyes. "We'll talk about this later," she said. "After church. Okay?"

"But until then, let's keep all this to ourselves,"

Dada added.

Wilber shifted uncomfortably in his booster seat. "Are we in trouble? We're not lying. I promise."

"Oh, sweetie. We know you're not lying," Mama said. She pointed to Dada. "Our first date was on Uncle Ned's island."

Edith was shocked. "It was?!"

"Yeah," Dada said, "but, guys, we really can't talk about Babylon now. They've been sneaking around Earth forever, so it's not safe to talk about it until we get home."

The children looked at each other. Edith could feel her hands starting to shake.

Dada flashed a confident smile. "What does the Bible say about fear?"

Wilber flopped back against his seat. "I don't either know," he whined.

"Yes, you do," Mama reassured him. "Do you think Shadrach, Meshach, and Abednego were scared?"

Edith avoided Mama's eyes and hid behind Ana's car seat.

"I don't know," Wilber finally answered. "Probably."

Dada nodded. "Of course, they were scared. But did they disobey God?"

"I guess not," Edith admitted, wiping tears with the sleeve of her shirt. "But I don't want Babylon to take us over." The thought was so terrible she couldn't hold back anymore. Tears fell heavily from her eyes.

"Oh, sweetheart," Mama said. "It's okay."

Dada pulled the van into the church parking lot, found a spot, and stopped the vehicle. He turned off the engine.

"But guys," Wilber roared. "If Babylon is already here, what're we going to do?!"

Everyone slowly unbuckled and left the van. Dada hugged Edith and Wilber at the same time. His voice was calm and loving. "Remember when you guys decided you wanted to follow Jesus?"

The children nodded, sniffling a little. Mama handed Ana to Edith and grabbed the diaper bag before shutting the van doors.

Dada put his arm around his children. "When you did that, God gave you the Holy Spirit. So, whatever happens in life, God will be with you. It doesn't matter if Babylon attacks or if Earth stays safe forever. Now come on. Grab your Bibles. We're late!"

Their parents led the way, and the children followed. Wilber leaned over to Edith and whispered. "If

Babylon comes, I'm afraid I won't be brave enough to fight them," he admitted. "Brave to follow Jesus, I mean."

"I know. Me too," Edith agreed, repositioning Ana on her hip. "What should we do?"

Ana slapped Wilber on the top of his head.

"What was that for?"

Ana looked Wilber in the eyes and growled.

Edith nodded. More than anyone else in the family, Edith could understand Ana best. "God will protect us," she said, pausing to think. "But even if he doesn't, Jesus has a mansion for us in heaven."

Wilber nodded. "Yeah!" he cheered. "I don't care how bad it gets. I won't worship Babylon."

Edith nodded. She looked up to the clouds for any sign of Babylon. There was nothing there. "Maybe we should start praying now," she said. "That way, if Babylon does come, we'll be ready."

CHAPTER

06

BIG OLD TRUNK

When the kids got home, they showed Mama and Dada where Sushi crashed. Although the shell was gone, it was clear something had happened.

"Follow me," Dada said, leading everyone to his bedroom. He went to the closet and opened the gun safe. It was tall enough to walk inside, and the children had never seen it open. As they looked on with amazement, Dada pulled out a large metal trunk. It had 4 padlocks, and the sides were covered with stickers that said things like "Beware of Venomous Beasts" and "Caution: Radioactive Material Inside."

Dada set the trunk on the bed. He wouldn't let the children see inside as he opened the lid. They could hear things clatter and bang around as he dug through the items, and at one point, Wilber was pretty sure he heard the tail of a rattlesnake.

"I can't wait to see what he's looking for," Edith whispered to Wilber, who nodded excitedly.

Eventually, Dada pulled out a bubble wand.

"Ah, man. Bubbles are so boring," Wilber groaned, rolling his eyes.

"Not these bubbles," Dada said.

With a gentle breath, he blew through the wand. A tiny bubble formed and grew until it touched the children and absorbed them. After a few seconds, the glossy orb filled the room and pressed against the wall. The whole family was inside. Even Rebel was there, trying to chew his way out.

"Babylon can't hear us in here," Mama explained. Her voice now had a strange echo.

Dada reached into the box and pulled out two rings. He showed them to his children. They looked exactly like the one Sushi wore, only these ones were colorless and dead.

"When we were your age," Dada explained. "We had

rings."

"All of this is hurting my brain," Edith said, trying to connect the dots.

"Well," Mama began, sitting on the edge of the bed. Ana sat on her lap. "I found mine inside a shooting star. It landed on Gigi and Papa's farm."

Edith and Wilber looked at each other. "Cool," they said. A second later, Ana copied them in her little baby voice, "Coooo."

Wilber stepped closer to his father. "How'd you get yours?"

"I got mine from a kangaroo wearing Hammer pants. He was drowning in the lake by Granny's house, and I saved him."

Wilber laughed. "What's hammer pants?"

"You're focusing on the wrong part of the story."

"How come you never told us about this?" Edith asked. "I feel like you lied to us. Or kept secrets. Or... I don't know."

"We had our reasons," Mama explained, putting her arm around Edith. "First, we didn't want Babylon to find out we were fighting against them. It could have put our family in danger."

"Secondly, our rings stopped working."

"Are they broken?" Edith asked.

Dada shrugged. "Mine turned grey after I decided to marry Mama."

"And mine stopped working when I was pregnant with Edith."

The lifeless rings sat in Dada's hand. Edith picked one up, and it instantly began to glow.

"Woah," everyone said at the same time.

Wilber quickly picked up the other. It also came back to life.

"Let me see that," Dada said, taking the ring back. The glowing metal instantly dimmed, and the light died. With a raised eyebrow, he dropped the ring back into Wilber's hand. It glowed once more.

Up until now, the children had viewed their trip to Ned with nervousness and fear. It had been an exciting experience, but it was also one they didn't want to relive. But that was changing. Their parents had not only been to the island... they had been heroes there! All three children felt their anxiety fade. A sense of adventure and purpose was calling to them.

"Does this mean we can go back?" Wilber asked.

"No!" Mama said quickly. "You're not old enough."

"Hold on a sec." Dada sat down next to Mama and

put his arm around her. Mama pushed him away.

"They aren't ready," Mama said. "Ana's just a baby."

Ana stood up on the bed. She pulled out her pacifier with one hand and then shoved the other hand into her mouth. Ana pulled out a ring and held it up. It also glowed brightly.

Dada was puzzled. "Where did that come from?"

"Is that Sushi's?" Edith asked, now a little annoyed. "Ana, that's stealing."

Mama was shaking. "No one's going back there," she said sternly. "We almost died... more than once."

"It wasn't so bad," Dada whispered softly.

Mama stared at him in disbelief. "You had your legs blown off."

"They grew back," he said, gently patting his knees. "I don't even have scars."

"Not physical ones," Mama quickly added. "But I know you still miss Teddy. And I know you'll never forget what happened to Baby Louis."

Dada nodded. "You're right."

"There are some things your heart will never *ever* forget," Mama said. "I'm not ready to put them through that."

Wilber started to whine. "Please let us go. Please.

Please. Pleeeeease."

Dada stood up. "Mama's right. Give me the rings."

The children obeyed, but doing so felt like betraying their hearts.

Dada reached for Ana's ring. "I want that one too."

"That's not fair," Edith said. "It's not even yours."

"It's not yours either," he said, locking all three in his trunk.

Wilber flopped on the bed like a toddler throwing a tantrum. Ana let out a loud, bloodthirsty cry.

"Everyone, stop freaking out," Dada said with a laugh. "We'll never let you go if you act like babies."

Edith quickly sat down on the bed with perfect posture. "We'll be good."

Wilber was slower to catch on but quickly mimicked his sister's behavior. "Yep. We won't be bad."

Ana let out another bloodthirsty cry, but Edith pulled her down and helped fold her hands. "Don't ruin this," Edith whispered.

"Kay," she nodded, a big frown on her face. "Ana, be good."

Dada was stern. "Don't talk about this again until Mama or I tell you it's safe." Dada pulled out the bubble wand and walked to the door. On the opposite end of the loop, there was a long needle. He poked the bubble, and it popped instantly.

A week went by before the parents gathered the family together again. Dada instructed everyone to be quiet until he put up a bubble.

"Alright," he said once everything was safe. "Mama and I don't think you're ready for this."

The children opened their mouths, about to whine, but Mama silenced them with a sharp stare.

"But if Babylon is here—and for an actual invasion this time—we can't hide you from what's coming."

Dada held Mama's hand. "We might only have a short time—hopefully, more—but there's a lot you'll need to learn. And you'll have to go a lot of it alone," Dada explained.

Mama nodded. "Dada and I did some tests with the rings, and even if someone else opens a portal, we can't go through. It won't even open if we are close."

"That's weird," Edith said. "I wonder why."

Dada shrugged. "Something magical is preventing us from going back."

"So… what are you talking about?" Wilber asked. When everyone turned to him, he blushed and hid the toy he had been playing with. "Sorry, I wasn't listening."

"I'm *talking about*," Dada said, pausing for dramatic effect, "letting you go back to Uncle Ned's."

The children cheered. "Thank you. Thank you. Thank you," they said.

"But," Dada quickly added, "there are rules."

"Whatever they are," Edith said quickly, "we'll do it."

Mama was stern. "Rule #1. Follow Jesus. Always. No matter what you see or anyone asks you to do, you do what God would want you to do."

All three children nodded excitedly.

Dada gave the next. "Rule #2: Homeworld Matters Most. That means, even if you were out adventuring all day, your grades and attitudes can't be bad at home... and you still have to do your chores. You can't leave puppy poop all over the backyard because adventuring made you tired."

Again, the children nodded.

"Rule #3: Protect Each Other," Mama said. "Never leave family behind. Don't fight with each other. If one of you falls, pick them up. You won't be good at adventuring if you don't have unity in your team. That includes Rebel."

Edith put an arm around her brother and her sister. Wilber hugged her side, and Ana leaned in. "We promise."

Dada put his hand on his belly. "Rule #4: Be Back For Dinner. We'll talk about what happened that day while we eat dinner, and Mama and I will give you advice."

Mama pointed at the kids. "If I'm going to be at home worrying all day, you have to tell us what's happening. So Rule #5: No Secrets."

Dada sat beside the children, and Mama sat on the other side.

"If you can agree to our rules," Dada said, "you can go adventuring."

Wilber punched the air. "Let's go!"

Ana copied him. "Yesh!"

"Thank you so much," Edith said as she hugged her parents. "You guys are the best."

Dada gave each of the children a ring.

"Now what?" Wilber asked.

Mama took a deep breath. "Go find a door."

"When you get there," added Dada, "go to the church and ask for help."

A few hours later, Edith let out a long sigh. The children were in the backyard, sitting around the sandbox. Their parents were inside cleaning up lunch. Edith's ring, which had once been Mama's, led them here.

Ana was about to eat her fourth shovel of sand when Edith pulled it out of her hands. "Gross, Ana."

"Me hab it," Ana said forcefully, spewing sand as she spoke. "Gib it, Eya!"

Edith rolled her eyes. "Fine," she said, letting go of the shovel.

Ana let Rebel lick the shovel before putting it back in her mouth.

"Are we ready?" Edith asked, turning back to the sandbox.

"Yep," Wilber said. "If bad fings are coming to Earth. I want to stop them."

Edith nodded. "Me too."

"Me," Ana said, raising her hand.

The children held out their hands, and all three rings glowed brightly. The light showed around them, pointing directly under their feet to the door they had already located.

"Let's dig until we find the portal," Wilber said.

All the kids pulled back sand. Even Rebel helped. A large piece of plastic was just a few inches under the surface.

"This wasn't here earlier," Edith said.

After a minute of moving sand, they revealed a large door. It looked like a giant plastic starfish used to make sand molds.

"I got this," Wilber exclaimed as he flipped the lid out of the sandbox.

Underneath the plastic was another magic portal. It was a swirling whirlpool made up of quicksand and stars.

Edith held out her arms, stopping everyone from diving in. "I think we should pray before we go."

Wilber nodded and clasped his hands. Ana copied him.

"Dear Jesus," Edith said. "Please keep us safe. Protect us. Help us learn how to protect our family and our home. We love you."

And all the children said, "Amen."

"So the first thing we need to do is—" But Edith was interrupted before she could remind everyone of the plan.

"Yay-hoo!" Wilber shouted as he jumped in.

Rebel quickly followed.

"Guys, wait," Edith begged.

Ana ignored her. She popped a pacifier in her mouth, gave her sister a double thumbs-up, and rolled into the portal.

Edith was now starting to feel a little nervous. She looked back at the house and saw her parents through the window. Their eyes were closed, and they were holding hands. Edith was sure they were praying for her. That gave her hope.

"I'm coming," she said to her siblings, jumping into the whirlpool.

CHAPTER 07
RIDING CRABBY

Wilber hit the stage and landed on his feet, and Ana skidded along the surface on her bottom. "Weeeee," she said with a clap. Edith landed with a stumble, but Wilber caught her before she fell.

"We're back on the island," Wilber said with a big smile.

They all felt wobbly, but Edith turned to the giant crab once the dizziness wore off. "Uncle Ned, we're back."

The giant eyes turned inward to the children. "Your world didn't fall already, did it?" he asked, rumbling the stage with his voice.

Wilber spoke with confidence, but only because his temper began to flare. "No, and it never will," he said. "I'm going to punch those bad guys in the butts."

"Wilber!" Edith snapped. "Sorry, Uncle Ned. How is Sushi?"

"Depends on what you mean," the crab admitted. "After she got better, she joined the Pirate's Guild. She's been trying to get revenge on the orcs who ruined her home."

"Can you take us to her? " Edith asked. "She says there are spies on our planet, and we need to know where they are."

Uncle Ned made a clicking sound with his mouth. "She's been going to some dangerous places," Ned confessed. "I don't think you'd survive."

"But we're awesome," Wilber argued. "We can handle it."

"No," Ned said.

Ana pointed to the city behind them. "Turt."

"Oh, right," Edith nodded. "How do we get to church?"

"Of which religion?" Uncle Ned asked.

Wilber rolled his eyes. "Jesus. Duh."

"Sorry, but that church doesn't exist anymore."

Edith's jaw dropped.

"The mob burned it down years ago."

Wilber threw his hands up. "Well, now what?"

Edith motioned for Wilber and Ana to come closer. They sat down in a circle as Rebel took turns licking their faces.

"None of our ideas are working," Wilber said.

Edith tapped her cheek as she thought. "Should we go home and ask what to do?"

Uncle Ned cleared his throat. "If it helps, you could go to the Orientation Building. They train new adventurers about living on my island. If I were you, I would start there."

"Cool," Edith said. "How do we do that?"

Uncle Ned's eyestalk bent backward. He motioned to a cobblestone road behind the stage. "Follow that path," he said. "When you get to the Depot, ask for a ride to the Orientation Building."

"Thankooee," Ana said.

"Yes, thank you very much," Edith agreed.

The kids left the stage and ran to the cobblestone road. Rebel hopped along the path, chasing and biting at the purple grasshoppers. Edith carried Ana, and they pointed and marveled at all the amazing things they saw.

On the right side of the path, there were fields of wheat. They were tall and swayed in the breeze. Caterpillars fat as buses cut through the grain like lawnmowers. Little goblins rode on top, wearing overalls and work gloves. When Wilber waved, one tipped his straw hat with a kind gesture.

There was a beach on the left side of the path. Dolphins jumped and caught fish in the shallows. Water stretched out a few miles before falling off the crab's body. Sasquatch surfed along the edge and did tricks on the rolling waves. A small island was across the sea and rested on Ned's right side.

The children followed the cobblestone road until it eventually ended at what looked like a train station. They walked up the stairs and looked around. The platform was covered by an overhang that shaded them from the hot sun. Benches lined the stone platform, and there was enough seating for 50.

On one bench, an astronaut sat reading a newspaper. On another, the ghost of a monkey sat. He was wearing a cowboy hat and a couple of six-shooters. The last bench was covered with gnomes. Although they were only a few inches tall, they argued loudly over the last bite of a candy bar.

There was a small building on the other end of the platform. It was about the size of a shed, and there was a little door and window. The sign above the window read, "Ticket Booth."

"Let's see if we can get a ticket," Edith said.

Wilber knocked on the shutters, and the windows swung open with a bang. A large golden robot appeared, and he was wearing a pinstripe suit.

"Whatta you want?" asked a familiar-sounding voice.

"Rustbeard?" Edith asked. "Is that you?"

The robot waved dismissively at the girl. "No. I'm Punchbucket," the robot said. He spoke fast and pulled out a pocket watch. "You've wasted 9 seconds of my life. What do you want?"

Edith blushed. "Sorry, you look just like someone we know."

"Of course I do," Punchbucket said, annoyed. "There's a Dittomark for every job there is. Same model, just a different person. Now tell me, 'WHAT DO YOU WANT?!'"

Wilber jumped back and then eventually laughed.

"Sor-ry!" he said sarcastically.

Edith quickly stepped in front of her brother. "We want to go to the Orientation Building. Do you know how to get there?"

Punchbucket never looked up from his pocket watch. "Of course I do. Do you have tickets?"

Wilber lifted his hands and shrugged. "We've never been here before."

Punchbucket's robotic face was unmoving and emotionless. Yet, his whole body trembled with frustration as he slumped in his chair. Faintly, just barely audible, the kids could hear him say, "I hate freeloaders."

Punchbucket stood up, walked over to the wall behind him, and looked around. Dozens of cubbies covered the back wall, and each one was filled with a different animal. Most were filled with different kinds of fish, but the kids spotted a few birds, jellyfish, and other small creatures.

Punchbucket grabbed a bright orange fish out of a hole at the top. He turned sharply and threw it out the window. Wilber bobbled it before eventually catching it.

"After this, you won't get another ride unless you pay," Punchbucket said. "Throw that fish on the tracks and get off my platform."

Wilber couldn't help but laugh. Edith quickly pushed her brother away from the ticket booth. "If you keep being difficult," she whispered to him, "you'll get us in trouble."

When they got to the platform, Wilber looked at the fish and shrugged. He tossed it on the track. Rebel howled mournfully, watching it with longing eyes.

Nothing happened.

"This fish is broken," Wilber shouted at Punchbucket. "Can we get a—"

The sound of clicking silenced him. Running to the depot, they saw a crab the size of their minivan. She sidestepped along the tracks with a dopey expression on her face.

"Baby one," Ana giggled.

The crab stopped at the platform and tossed the fish into her mouth. After a few seconds, she burped out the bones. Two baseball-sized eyes turned toward the children. "All aboard," she said as a stepladder rolled off her side.

Wilber climbed on first. He reached down, and Edith tried to lift Ana to him. The baby refused help and awkwardly pulled herself up, whining loudly if anyone tried to help her. After what felt like forever, Ana got up and sat on the floor next to the ladder. Rebel jumped up, and Edith climbed in after.

On top of the crab, there was a large, curved sofa. It started at the left eye, circled around the body, ending at the right eye. There were enough seats for 4-6 people.

"Choo choo!" the crab said, making a train sound as she took off down the tracks.

Wilber slid along the sofa until he was next to one of the eyes. "Are you an animal like Uncle Ned?"

"I'm a titan," the crab explained. "And Uncle Ned is my actual uncle. He saved us when we were babies, so now we help him move stuff."

Wilber frowned. "Hey! We're not stuff!"

The crab leaped off the train tracks and onto another cobblestone road. They hit the ground hard, violently shaking the crab's whole body. Powerless to stay in their seats, the kids bounced onto the floor. As the crab continued to make turns at breakneck speeds, they rolled around like candies in a bowl.

On a straight stretch of road, Edith searched the sofa. Eventually, she found seatbelts. "Here," she said, buckling Ana in before herself.

Once everyone was securely in their seats, the ride

was far more enjoyable. The jumps reminded them of tubing at Johnson Lake, and they laughed as if they were merely ramping waves.

At first, Rebel whimpered at Edith's feet. Eventually, he grew confident and crawled onto the crab's flat head. The puppy lifted his head high into the air. His tongue hung out of his mouth, flinging dog spit all over the children. The spit would have further reminded them of the lake—that is—if the liquid wasn't sticky and didn't smell like a dumpster.

"That's nice you get to work with family," Edith said, trying to be polite. She put her hand over her mouth to keep dog spit from flying in.

"Yeah," the crab laughed. "Nicer than being eaten by Babylon!"

Wilber watched the countryside disappear as the crab carried them into the city. She jumped on a few rickety shops before leaping onto a glass skyscraper.

"Will you grow as big as Uncle Ned?" Edith asked.

The crab only stopped making train sounds when she spoke. "I hope. Big and strong. Like Uncle Ned. But I'll have to live another 100 million years first. Choo choo!" she said. "Chugga chugga chug-ga!"

The crab continued to climb up the skyscraper until

they got halfway up. A portion of the building opened up like a garage door.

"This is your destination," she said. The seat belts suddenly popped off, and the crab's claw grabbed Wilber by the shirt. She lifted him off her back and into the building. Gently, the crab set Wilber on a desk. Rebel jumped off before the crab finished unloading the girls.

"Bye-bye," the crab said, pushing off from the building with a giant leap. She disappeared into the clouds, and the building wall closed behind her.

Wilber looked around, frowning. "Aw, man," he complained, crawling off the desk and into the seat. "Are we in school?"

"Pay attention," snapped an old woman. The voice was stern and slimy.

CHAPTER
08
ADVENTURE CLASS

"Where is she?" Wilber asked, scanning the room. They were surrounded by empty desks. The opening in the wall had now disappeared entirely. Everything was white, sleek, and futuristic. An expensive-looking projector hung from the ceiling.

When they finally found the teacher, they were shocked. They expected her appearance to match the room. Something like a Space Admiral or time-traveling scientist. Instead, they found a wrinkly old squid. She was a little larger than the ones they'd seen at the zoo, but the tentacles were much longer. Still, she looked nothing like a teacher. She looked more like a curly mess of pink seaweed.

Yet the pile rose, pushing herself off the floor with her tentacles. When standing, she was almost as tall as Edith. Her slimy skin was covered in suction cups and liver spots. She wore a curly pink wig and glasses. "I am Professor Rhonda T. Plink," she said, staring at them with a single sleepy eye. "You may call me Professor Rhonda or Madame Plink. If you want your diploma, pay attention."

Wilber spoke without thinking. "Pay attention to what?" he asked in an obnoxiously rude tone. Although Wilber tried hard to be good, and even though his heart was often in the right place, he couldn't be polite to save his life... especially in school. More often than not, the boy found himself in the "Be Still" chair until he could calm down.

Edith, on the other hand, was always diplomatic. "To our teacher, of course."

This seemed to ease the growing frustration on Rhonda's face. The color of her skin faded from a bright red to a rosy white as she moved slowly across the room. When she got to the front, a feeble and shaky tentacle rose to the ceiling. Once she reached the dangling hook, she pulled. Her whole body lifted off the ground before the projector screen finally came down. Another tentacle shakily pushed a button against the wall. The lights turned off, and the projector came on.

Cheesy music filled the room. It sounded like a cartoon that taught babies about colors and shapes. Ana liked the music. She danced by twisting her hands at the wrists and wiggling her hips. Rebel was already asleep under Wilber's desk.

A picture of space filled the screen.

"Welcome to the United Federation of Guilds," the voice said. Their logo appeared over a starry sky. The video often glitched before continuing, and even the music sputtered. "For g-g-generations, the UFG has been on the frontlines of the war – the war – the war against Great Babylon."

Edith leaned over and whispered to her brother. "This video looks really old. Like one of Dada's tape movies for the VCR."

"Yeah," Wilber agreed. "Like 100 million infinities old."

The elderly octopus adjusted her glasses with one tentacle and pointed to the children with another. "Pay attention," Rhonda said, repositioning the wig on her slimy head. "If you want a diploma, you must pay attention."

Next, the video showed a dozen troops entering the battlefield, triumphantly defeating scary monsters. The woman's voice continued. "If you are watching this video, you are likely orphans of a world destroyed by Great Babylon... or about to be-be-be," the dialogue sputtered and then cut out completely. The screen stopped on one of the soldiers. He was frozen awkwardly in place, but when the video started back up again, he flashed a smile and winked. "Or maybe you just want some sweet, sweet loot. Am I right?"

One of the soldiers in the video stabbed a monster in the stomach with a spear, which instantly exploded into gold coins and gemstones.

"We get treasure?" Wilber exclaimed. His mouth hung open. "So cool."

"Yeah, so tool," Ana copied.

But Edith had a worried expression. She slowly lifted her hand. "Uh, if I get stabbed, will I explode like that?"

"Pay attention," Rhonda screeched.

The screen now showed a younger version of Professor Rhonda. Her skin was smooth and more colorful. Her hair was long and soft, and instead of glasses, she wore a triangle scarf.

"I'm sure you're asking yourself, 'But why should I-I-I-I join the UFG?' The answer is simple: you'll die without Uncle Ned's protection. And all you have to do in return is help us fight Babylon. So no matter who you want to be, we can help."

The video transitioned to images of the city on Uncle Ned's back. The younger version of Rhonda posed fashionably on the screen. "If you can imagine it," she said, "our guilds can help you become it."

The screen was then filled with a dozen robots that looked like Punchbucket and Rustbeard. "For every job, there is a Dittomark Robot. They're waiting to train you, so that means new skill-ill-ill-ills."

Next, they were shown large purple birds. They were as big as pigs, looking and acting like they had no brains. One tried to eat the fence post, and another was trying to stand on its own head. The young Rhonda explained what they saw, "For every species, there is a Dooply-Bird to teach you their abilities."

An ugly cave troll stepped into view. He was wearing a white jacket and safety goggles. With an electric pole, he pushed a moose toward one of the

Dooply-Birds. When the two touched, the bird turned into a purple moose. The cave troll then gave the camera a thumbs up. The word "science" flashed across the screen.

"And for every Homeworld," Rhonda continued, "there is a ticket to go explore." The next scene showed a dozen green children on a dry and dusty planet. They had long antennae and entered a spaceship. A second later, they were getting off and exploring a world filled with incredible natural wonders.

"Oh, I want to go there," Edith said to Ana, but her sister wasn't paying attention. She was hanging off her desk chair, trying to pet Rebel.

"All you have to do is complete quests and earn points called Street Cred. These credits can be used to purchase weapons, spells, and vehicles from our shops. Also, as you complete missions, you-you-you'll get stronger and level up."

Wilber nodded excitedly. "Ooooh! That's what we need."

"So get out there, brave Adventurer. Fight for your glory. Fight for riches and the dreams you have." The music rose in the background, and even though the poor quality made the sound wobble, it was like the ending of an epic movie. "While we will never be able to defeat Great Babylon, at least we can have fun before we die-die-die-die-die-die."

As the video continued to skip, Edith turned to Wilber. "Well, that's frightening," she whispered. Her brother nodded, his eyes wide.

The young version of Rhonda on the screen was charming. She laughed and moved with grace as she talked. When the video ended, the lights turned back on. The current version of Rhonda appeared in the same place, grumpy and old.

"AH!" Wilber screamed.

Edith raised her hand. "Thank you for showing us... that," she said. "But how do you find spies?"

Rhonda was asleep on her feet, and the question startled her awake. "Pay attention," she screeched, again fixing her appearance with her tentacles.

"But the movie's over," Wilber explained, pointing to the screen.

"Oh," she said, collapsing to the ground behind the desk. "Of course it is."

They couldn't see her, but they could hear her. Suction cups made popping sounds as she pulled herself along the floor, closer and closer to where the children were sitting. Her movements were slow. Painfully slow.

"Can I help carry you?" Edith asked.

Rhonda didn't say anything. She just kept pulling herself forward... pop pop pop... slap... slide... pop pop pop... slap... slide.

When Rhonda finally got to the children, she rolled up onto her tentacles and stood up. She gave each child a piece of paper, leaving squid juice all over their hands.

"Groooosss!" Wilber said.

Edith elbowed him in the side. Wilber changed his facial expression and said, "I mean, fank you." He held up the soggy diploma and tried to read the words. It was in some language he didn't recognize, which still could have been English, as he wasn't that good at reading yet. The more he looked at it, the more liquid rolled onto his hands and arms.

"Uh, guys," Wilber said, trying desperately to wipe the squid juice from his hands. The more he struggled, the more he got it everywhere else. Before long, slime was on his shirt, pants, and hair. "I fink I need hannatizer."

"What do you think hand sanitizer would do to my skin?" Rhonda snorted. "It would kill me!" She collapsed back to the ground and slowly pulled herself to the desk.

"Wait," Edith protested. "How do we find the spies on our planet."

The squid woman sighed, ignoring Edith's question. "There aren't many humans left on Ned. I could only find one willing to be your mentor... and he's not very good. Actually, he's pretty much terrible."

"Aw, man," Wilber said, folding his arms. As he moved, squid juice flung across the room.

"At least he's human," Edith said, reassuring her brother. "He'll want to save Earth as much as we do."

The squid woman pointed three tentacles to the door. "He's waiting outside, so it would be great if you could leave now. I have to clean the room. You got human dust on everything. Nasty."

Wilber, still dripping with squid juice, stood with his jaw dropped. "Nasty?" he asked, pointing to the slime dripping from his hand. As he did this, Rebel lapped up the long string of slimy goop.

"Stop picking fights," Edith scolded Wilber. "We're supposed to be back for dinner, and we haven't really done anything yet." She picked up Ana and walked to the door. Rebel jogged beside her.

"Fine," Wilber said, running to catch up.

Edith stepped out of the room, turned, and her face went pale. She let out a loud scream. "There's a monster out here," she cried.

CHAPTER

09

CREEPY CUPCAKE

Wilber whipped around the corner to find something he'd never seen before. A living skeleton was standing right before him. There was no skin, muscles, or flesh on his body. White pearl bones in strange clothing. Eyes hovering in pitch black sockets.

"Get away from them," Wilber screamed, jumping between the monster and his sisters. He pulled back his fist, ready to punch the skeleton in his boney face.

But the skeleton did something none of them expected. He shrieked!

The child-sized skeleton shrunk back, and his

boney fingers lifted to protect his face. "Don't hit me," he begged. "I'm your mentor."

Wilber instantly relaxed. Edith stopped screaming.

"But... our mentor was supposed to be human."

The skeleton readjusted his rotten clothes, and a handful of dust fell on the floor. "I *am* human," he explained, a little defensive. "Just cursed."

"Sorry," Edith said, a little ashamed for reacting so poorly. "We've never seen a skeleton before."

"Wow!" Wilber exclaimed. "How did you get cursed."

"I was in Grubbie's Dungeon, and a chubby little warlock got me."

"That sounds terrible," Edith comforted.

The skeleton shrugged. "It was my fault," he admitted. "I ran out of spell block. Should have been more careful."

Edith watched a spider build a web from the skeleton's shoulder to his jaw. "Is there anything you can do?" she asked.

"Not that I've found," he admitted. "Good news is, now that I'm already a little dead, I'm almost impossible to kill."

"What's the bad news?" Wilber asked.

The skeleton lifted his shirt. There were three arrows stuck in his ribcage. "Every time I go on raids, I keep getting stuff lodged in my body. No matter how hard I try, I can't wiggle it free." He grabbed one of the arrows and shook it violently. It just rattled around the inside of his boney chest.

Edith stuck out her tongue and gagged.

"Cool!" her brother exclaimed. "My name is Wilber, and these are my sisters. This is Edith, and this is Ana. Our dog's name is Rebel."

"My name is Stan, but everyone calls me Cupcake."

Wilber burst out laughing. "That's a funny name for a skeleton!"

Cupcake nodded. "Yeah, I almost unlocked the Baker job class before this happened." He pointed to his boney face. "I was going to open up a little bakery here on Ned, but as it turns out, no one wants to eat anything made by someone who looks like me. Not even other skeletons."

"Bummer," Wilber said. "Sorry, I laughed."

"It's okay," Cupcake replied, putting his arm around Wilber. "I transferred my leftover XP to Potions, so I'm an Alchemist now."

Wilber nodded as Cupcake led them to the elevator.

"Cupcake," Edith said, "we've heard that Babylon might try to invade Earth. Can these diplomas help us protect our planet?"

The elevator doors opened, revealing a large metal box. Edith examined it closely as everyone walked inside. Scratches covered the walls, making her wonder if it was still safe to ride. She even saw a dent that looked suspiciously like a dinosaur footprint. Once everyone was in, Cupcake hit the button that said "Lobby."

"Unfortunately, no," Cupcake said. "The Federation likes to pretend they're standing up to Great Babylon, but in all honesty, we're more like flies in cookie dough. They make it taste a little gross, but it doesn't stop me from eating them."

"Uh, what's that mean?" Wilber asked.

"If Babylon wants Earth, they'll eventually get it."

"How can you be so calm about that?" Edith interjected. "It's your home too, you know."

Cupcake put his boney fingers against his chest. "Oh," he admitted. "I'm human, but I'm from a different Earth than you are."

Edith shot him a puzzled look.

Cupcake held up two fingers. Both looked similar,

but one had a crack down the middle. "There are a million Earths," he explained, raising one finger at a time until all of them were up. Each of Cupcake's fingers had a different dent or deformity. "But every Earth is different—some a little different, some a lot different."

Wilber's jaw dropped in surprise.

"My world was taken over by giant roly-polies. Everyone now lives in a walled city where Montana used to be. So who knows?" Cupcake asked. "When your world falls apart, maybe you can still live there. If you survive. And if it doesn't fully fall apart."

Wilber shook his head and clenched his jaw. "We're trying to find help, and everyone just keeps telling us we're going to die," Wilber exploded. His face was flushed with red hot anger. Edith put her arm on his shoulder, but he shrugged it off. "Everyone keeps saying it's hopeless, but I'm not giving up."

Cupcake nodded. "Don't worry," the skeleton said. "I'll be the best mentor I can. It might be hopeless, but I'll do everything possible to help. We can get some equipment, do some quests, and earn loot."

Wilber eased up. He wiped the tears from his eyes with the palms of his hands. "Thank you."

"That's very nice of you," Edith added.

"Don't mention it," Cupcake said. "Now, let's get down to business."

They emerged from the elevator and entered a large and empty lobby. The only person in the room was a receptionist at the front desk. She was a Dittomark robot, talking loudly on the phone. "And that's when I told Mabel to leave the bum," the robot said in a nasal voice. "She can do so much better, and besides, she needs to focus on her career."

Cupcake clapped his hands, but the bones made a clicking sound. "Do you wanna get jobs?"

"Yuck, no," Wilber said. "That's not fun."

Edith elbowed her brother hard in the side. "Sorry, Cupcake, we'll do whatever you think will help us, but we can't tonight. Our parents want us home for dinner."

Wilber rubbed his side, exaggerating the pain. "I'm gonna tell Mama," he whispered.

"That's okay," Cupcake said, leading everyone outside the Orientation Building.

The city was full of creatures, and the buildings were taller than any they had seen back home. Not even the Nebraska state capital was as tall as these. Between the buildings, everyone was packed in, shoulder to shoulder.

"It reminds me of being downtown on Husker game day," Wilber said.

Cupcake led them down the sidewalk to the corner. "There's a place to call a crab just over here," he said, pointing to the corner. "I think I have a ticket, too."

Cupcake dug around in his apron. It had well-worn pockets along the front, and he checked them all before finally pulling something out. "Here we go," he said, revealing a banana-sized shrimp. He tossed it in the street.

Again, Rebel looked longingly at the food. He whined as both Edith and Wilber held him back.

Within seconds, they could hear clicking crab legs. It appeared on the side of the building, took a swan dive, and landed right in front of them.

"This guy will get you home," Cupcake said with a toothy grin. "Can you guys hang out tomorrow?"

"I fink so," Wilber nodded. "But we need your help finding a friend. Her name is Sushi, and Uncle Ned said she's always fighting with pirates."

"I have a friend who works at the docks," Cupcake said. "I'll ask if he knows when she'll be back. If not by tomorrow, I'll give you a tour and show you around Ned. Sound good?"

Everyone nodded, even Rebel.

After the children thanked Cupcake and said their goodbyes, they crawled into the seats. Almost as soon as they sat down, the crab took off. He jumped, ran, and went through a dozen portals before arriving in their backyard. The kids unloaded, and as soon as they did, the crab disappeared through another portal.

"Dada, they're back," Mama hollered. She must have been waiting on the back deck for them to return. She ran down the stairs and hugged them all.

By the time Dada stepped onto the deck, everyone was already sitting around the patio table. "I've spent all morning Babylon-proofing our house," he explained. "It wasn't as hard as Ana-proofing, but it wasn't easy. The good news is: we should be able to talk freely—even without a bubble."

"Cool!" Wilber exclaimed. He cupped his hands around his mouth and shouted to the sky. "Great Babylon has a big butt!"

Ana copied her brother, yelling, "Pig putt," with her hands cupped over her mouth.

Without meaning to, Edith and Mama both shook their heads. Their movements were perfectly synced as if they had done this before. Because they had. Many times.

"You're being a bad influence," Edith told Wilber. "You need to be more responsible."

Wilber stuck out his tongue.

"Enough," Dada said, stepping between the two and changing the subject. "I had fun going through my old stuff, and now the house is safer."

"And dinner is ready. I've got it warming in the stove," Mama said, standing up. "I'll bring it out here, and you can tell us about your trip."

Edith stood up quickly. "I can help you set the table," she offered.

"That would be wonderful," Mama said.

Edith arranged plates and silverware as Mama came outside with food. There were chicken breasts for the parents and chicken nuggets for the kids. Mama also brought out multiple side dishes, most of which were healthy foods that made Wilber gag.

"Fries?!" Ana shouted, searching the table until she found them. "Me fries."

"We know," Edith said, putting a handful of french fries on her sister's plate.

Ana blew a kiss to Edith before shoving a handful of fries into her mouth."

Dada prayed for the meal and then turned to the children. "So, how was your adventure?"

"Dada, it was so much fun," Wilber shouted.

The children shared stories about what they had seen and done as they ate. By the time dinner was finished, the kids had told the entire story, not leaving anything out.

Eventually, Dada turned to Mama. "It sounds like a lot has changed since we were there," he said. "I can't believe they burned the church down."

"That has me a little worried," Mama admitted. "They've always hated humans, but I don't remember anyone having a problem with the church."

Dada turned back to the children. "What are you going to do next?" he asked as if they were in school and he was the teacher.

"How are we supposed to know?" Wilber asked. "We're just kids."

"Yeah," Edith said. "You're the grown-ups."

"Yeh," Ana said, tipping her plate onto the floor. Rebel ate the food so fast that no one could prevent the dog from lapping it up.

"We know this is confusing," Mama said, "but that's why we're doing this. We're here to help."

"But we won't always be," Dada explained. "So think about it. What would you do if we weren't here to give you the answers?"

Wilber slumped into his chair. "I wish there was still a church on Uncle Ned," Wilber said. "We could ask the pastor for help."

Mama nodded. "That doesn't help you now, but maybe you could plant a new church someday."

Edith leaned forward. As she thought, she played with her food, stirring what was left. "If we can't find Sushi, and if there's no church," she said with a sigh. "Then we need Cupcake to show us how to get stronger."

"But Cupcake just wants us to do chores," Wilber said, throwing his hands up before letting them fall back down. "I don't want a job. We need to learn how to fight. And we need weapons and stuff."

Mama smiled. "Buddy, on Uncle Ned, jobs give you powers and abilities. That's how you learn new stuff and get stronger. It's different from the jobs here on Earth."

"But there's also nothing wrong with working hard at a normal job," Dada quickly interjected.

"Oh, I want an Uncle Ned job super bad," Wilber

said, ignoring his father. "I want a job right now."

After dinner, the children brushed their teeth and went into Edith's room. "Will you guys tell us a story?" Edith asked.

"Yeah," Wilber agreed. "About the sword in Uncle Ned's back."

Mama crawled into Edith's bed, and the children cuddled around her. Ana fell asleep instantly.

"Well, no one really knows the full story," Mama informed them. "Uncle Ned won't tell anyone, but they say he was betrayed by a giant red panda named Wackadoo."

Wilber laughed. "That's a funny word."

Dada sat down on the edge of the bed. "Uncle Ned is a Titan, and there are other creatures as big as him," he explained. "They start off small, but the longer they live, the bigger they get. There are even some worlds so big—everyone there is a titan. Uncle Ned lived on a planet like that, and, a long, long time ago, Wackadoo attacked it."

Mama brushed Edith's hair. "Wackadoo destroyed and killed everything he could, but Ned gathered all his nieces and nephews during the attack. Right as Uncle

Ned jumped through a portal, Wackadoo stabbed him in the back. Ned went through, taking the sword with him but leaving Wackadoo to destroy the rest of his planet."

"Uncle Ned got all the baby crabs to safety," Dada explained. "But legend says Wackadoo has been hunting for Ned ever since. Promising to get his sword and his revenge."

"Wow," Wilber said. "Spooky."

"Now, it's bedtime," Mama said. "Say your prayers and go to sleep."

Wilber jumped up, excited. "Oh, I can't wait to get special powers tomorrow!"

CHAPTER

PILES OF LOOT

Early the following day, the children got ready and used their rings to find another portal.

"Portals are always shifting," Dada explained. "They're never in the same place twice, and that's why you need a ring. Without a ring, they're almost impossible to find."

The one they found was inside their neighbor's birdbath. They crawled in but did not get wet. Instead, they were taken directly to Uncle Ned. Wilber was still finishing his frozen waffle when he landed on the metal stage.

Cupcake was already there waiting for them. "Hello, friends," he said. "I called us a crab, so we're ready to go."

"Thank you," Edith said, crawling up the stairs to the seats. She buckled up Ana and then sat next to her sister. "I'll be glad when you can walk better, Ana. My arms are getting tired from carrying you."

"No. No," Ana growled in her best Mama voice.

Rebel followed Cupcake, and Wilber got on last. As soon as the skeleton sat down, the puppy began gnawing on Cupcake's shin bone as if it were a chew toy.

"No, Rebel!" Edith shouted, trying to pull the labrador back. "That's so rude!"

Cupcake waved her off with his hand. "It's okay," he said, and with a twist, he detached his leg at the knee. He tossed it down to Rebel, "I have the Regenerate ability. I'll just grow another or reattach it later."

"Bood-boy," Ana said as Rebel slobbered all over the bone.

"That's so cool," Wilber said. "How long does it take?"

"About an hour, but I can only do it once a day." Cupcake motioned for the crab to move. "I want to show you a few things before we get started."

As the crab entered the city, the children marveled at all the activity. There were flying machines of all kinds. Some were spaceships, some were boats with wings, and others were hot air balloons. There were also giant birds, dragons, and flying whales.

Eventually, the crab stopped at the tallest building on the island. Not only was the building enormous, but the giant sword was plunged through the center of it. It was the same sword they saw far away from the stage.

"It's over a mile to the top," Cupcake said, pointing straight up. They all cranked their heads back to see the end of the sword. "There's a watchtower and space station on the hilt."

"Wow," Wilber said, following the sword back down to the building. "It looks like the sword in the stone… only it's huge-mungus."

"Our parents told us about this," Edith explained. "About Wackadoo."

Cupcake pointed to the building at the base of the sword. "That's the Capital Building," he explained. "Whenever something important happens, everyone goes here. Every world, species, and guild comes to the capital to find out what our leaders have to say."

Next, Cupcake took them through the Market. There

were streets and streets filled with stores and shops. Some were as big as a mall, while others were barely more than a little stand on the sidewalk.

Cupcake motioned all around him. "Here, you can buy anything," he explained. "Swords, dynamite, flying saucers, diamonds, magic rings, pet dragons, hurricanes, nuclear reactors, mercenaries—literally anything you can think of."

"Wow," Wilber said, "that guy is selling dinosaurs."

Edith pointed at another shop. "I wonder how much those princess crowns are."

The last stop was at Adventurer Hall. It was a large dome surrounded by a staircase that circled the building. There were no walls on the outside—just pillars. Large groups were coming in and out of the building, but most creatures were just sitting on the steps, talking.

When the crab stopped, Cupcake stood up. By this point, his leg had already regenerated. "If you really want to stop Babylon," he said, holding his hands up to the building, "this is where you'll spend most of your time."

"Can we get jobs here?" Wilber asked, getting off the crab.

"Yep. It's also where you'll sign up for missions," Cupcake explained. "Follow me."

The children followed their skeleton friend up the stairs to an open plaza. Massive stone columns surrounded them, and they held up the dome.

"There are so many people," Edith marveled.

"The best part is," Cupcake said, "if you stay long enough, you might even see a celebrity. All the heroes hang out here: Razorface, Lady Dumptruck, Crowbar, Chad—all of them."

Wilber laughed. "Who are they?"

After they walked past the perimeter of pillars, they were inside the dome.

"They are the best adventurers alive. Razorface is even in the hall of fame," Cupcake said, pointing to the giant banners that hung inside the dome. There were thousands, all as wide as a road. Each showed a different hero, and written under their pictures were career stats.

"Are you up there?" Edith asked.

Cupcake laughed awkwardly. "I wish. These people are the strongest fighters in the UFG... ever. There hadn't been a new banner for over a hundred years, and then Razorface showed up. He's the greatest hero of our generation."

Cupcake admired the banners for a few more moments. He took a deep sigh and then motioned forward. "Come on," he said. "We can't stand and look at banners all day."

Cupcake led the children through the crowd. "This is where you sign up for missions and quests," Cupcake explained. "I wonder why it's so busy today."

While they stood there, a tall giraffe walked up. He wore post-apocalyptic armor and carried a baseball bat covered with barbed wire.

Cupcake waved. "Hey, Pete, what's going on?" he asked, motioning to the hubbub surrounding them.

"Another homeworld fell to Babylon this morning," Giraffe Pete said. "The Senate is doubling loot for anyone that can help relocate survivors."

"That's scary," Edith said.

Giraffe Pete looked at the children and turned back to Cupcake. "Do you want to ditch these guys and join my squad? We could use a healer. I already got Flip Flapjackie and Tiki Pterodactyl."

"Sorry, not this time," Cupcake explained, pointing to the children. "I got new recruits. Showing them around."

Pete the Giraffe smirked as he walked away.

Ana pointed to a large screen on the wall. It was bigger than four movie theater screens stacked on top of each other. The display was bright and flashy, even though hardly anyone looked at it. A list of names cycled through, each with numbers next to them.

"What's that?" Edith asked.

"That's the Yearly Rankings," Cupcake said, moving the children along. He led them through the crowds of people to the other side of the room. "The board only shows the top 100, though. Getting your name up there—even for one month—makes you like a celebrity. Stay in the top 100 for long enough, and you might even get your picture on one of those banners."

Next, Cupcake led them to a room opposite the screen. Piles of weapons and armor lined the walls and were scattered across the floor.

"It's like Santa's workshop," Wilber said, "only for fighting stuff."

"Look it over," Cupcake explained, moving a football helmet with his foot. "See how it feels in your hands. Once you find something, I'll sign you up for whatever job goes with that stuff. Also, I found out the Federation gave you a little Street Cred for helping

Sushi, so that will buy your first gear."

"That was nice of them," Edith said excitedly. "But these things all look so expensive! Will we have enough money if we each get something?"

Wilber was already up to his knees, excitedly digging through a pile of armor.

"Actually, this stuff should be pretty cheap," Cupcake guessed. "They're the leftovers from when a low-level adventurer dies."

Wilber stuck out his tongue, letting a bunch of cherry bombs fall out of his hands. "Gross! A dead guy touched these?" he said, making an exaggerated gagging sound. "I fink I'm gonna frow up."

"Wait. What?" Edith asked. "The people who used these weapons... died?!"

"Um, yeah," Cupcake said, a little uneasy. He was looking at a small black cauldron. "People die here a lot. All the time, actually. Most adventurers don't make it a month. Either that or they quit. Actually, I probably would have quit a long time ago if I didn't hate being home so much."

Ana picked up a sword twice her size and repeatedly banged it against the ground. The sound echoed loudly, and she only stopped after the metal floor cracked.

Cupcake cautiously took a step back. He then tossed Ana a belt made of dinosaur bones. "This boosts your strength stat when equipped with a broad sword."

Ana caught the belt with her mouth. Edith walked over and crouched down. She pulled the belt from Ana's mouth and helped her put it on. When Edith took a step back, she bumped into a large black hat.

"What's this?" she asked, pulling the hat out from under a pile of nunchucks. She set it on her head and examined her reflection in a full-sized shield. The brim was almost as wide as a sombrero, but it fit perfectly.

"Looking good, gurl," Wilber said, digging through another pile of items.

"I could be a wizard… like Gandalf," she said, pulling out a tall staff. Embedded in the wood was a white crystal. It looked like a star had exploded all over the top. She held it up beside her. The staff was a little bigger than she was.

"Wizard," Cupcake said. "Good choice. It looks like the baby's going Barbarian."

Ana continued to swing her sword around. The magic belt was wrapped around her pajama onesie, giving her the ability to wield it quite well. She could now easily swing a sword twice her size—and twice as heavy.

"Cool," Wilber said, pulling a futuristic rifle from the pile. "This looks like it's from a videogame."

"Good choice: Heavy Gunner," Cupcake explained. "Heavy on the firepower, and heavy on the... heavy."

The rifle had a strap, so Wilber let it hang on his shoulder. He then pulled out two sets of bird wings. "What are these for?"

Cupcake looked at them for a couple seconds. "They're for double jumping. You put them on your shoes."

Wilber slapped the wings on his dinosaur rain boots. He then jumped as high as he could. When he was at the highest, he jumped again. Feathers surrounded his feet as he leaped across the room.

"So cool," Wilber said, jumping again. But this time, he wasn't able to. "Ah, man. I fink they're broken."

Cupcake pointed to the boots. The feathers were all gone. Only goose-pimply buffalo wings were left. "They have a cooldown period. You have to wait until all the feathers grow back before you can use it again."

Already, Wilber could see little baby feathers sprouting across the skin. "Gross. And cool."

"How many credits do we have left?" Edith asked. "I want to get Rebel something."

Cupcake pulled a tablet out of his apron. It looked half like a computer, half a cookbook. His boney finger clicked on the screen as he entered the items. "Let's see. After the staff, hat, sword, belt, boots, and gun," he said, waiting for the cookbook to calculate. "Wow, that's a good deal. Depending on the price, you could still get a few more things."

Edith walked over to a pile of leather objects, primarily clothes. However, a small saddle lay on top. She picked it up and examined the item from all sides. "Here, boy," she said to Rebel.

The puppy was chewing on a pair of gloves but perked up as soon as his name was called. Rebel galloped to Edith, his big paws clobbering the items on the floor.

"Good boy," Edith said, scratching his head. Once the puppy calmed down, she bent over and strapped the saddle to his back. "Stay."

Rebel stood patiently as Edith lowered Ana onto the saddle. Once seated, Ana leaned forward and kissed Rebel on the back of the head. "Bood-boy," she said lovingly.

Edith put her hands on her hips, satisfied. "Now, I won't have to carry you anymore."

Ana moved the sword over her head to her back. It clung to her shoulders as if magnetized, and her hands were free to scratch Rebel's neck.

"Good finking, Edith!" Wilber shouted. "Should we get him something else?"

"Rebel," Edith said, pointing to a pile of items, "you pick something."

Rebel took off. Ana giggled as the dog jumped across the room. He leaped into a pile of items and disappeared until both he and Ana came out on the other side. He was wearing a new collar, and Ana looked a little dizzy.

"Good choice," Cupcake said. "The dash belt will help him run super fast."

Wilber gave Ana a high five. "We have all the powers now. Let's do this fing!"

Cupcake looked at his tablet. "You still have some creds left over, but not much. I suggest saving it."

Edith nodded in agreement.

Cupcake gathered the three children around him. "Last chance to trade something out. Everyone happy with what they got?" he asked.

All four nodded.

Suddenly, music filled the air, and confetti rained down. The children couldn't tell where it was coming from. A loud and epic voice boomed through the room. "New adventurers take the field." As the voice continued, written words appeared over each of them.

Edith: "Level 1 Wizard."

Wilber: "Level 1 Heavy Gunner."

Ana: "Level 1 Barbarian."

Rebel: "Level 1 Familiar"

The children looked around, wide-eyed. "What in the name of the law was that?" Wilber asked.

"It's fanfare," Cupcake explained.

"What's that?"

The skeleton shrugged. "No one knows where it comes from, but it tracks your XP and celebrates your achievements."

Edith rolled her eyes. "Really? No one knows?"

Cupcake held up his hands. "Don't look at me. Everyone pretty much just goes with it. Anyway," the skeleton said, clapping his boney hands together. "Eventually, we'll have to register each of you with a guild... but they give you a year to do that, so I suggest waiting."

"Eat," Ana cried, patting her tummy. "Me. Fries."

Cupcake was distracted and didn't hear her. "We still need to formally create a squad to start taking missions. You save on taxes if you register," he explained. Using his boney fingers, he began to count to himself. "You four, plus me, is five. We need six."

Wilber nodded excitedly. "Let's ask Sushi to join."

"Me! Fries! Now!" Ana screamed.

Everyone was startled. After a few moments, Edith spoke. "We should go home for lunch," she said, turning to Cupcake. "Would you like to come to our house and eat with us?"

Cupcake smiled but avoided making eye contact. "Sure," he said. "No one's ever invited me to their house before."

CHAPTER

11

PVP ARENA

"You can sit here," Edith said, pulling out a chair for Cupcake.

Dada handed Cupcake a plate and silverware. He had a curious look in his eyes. "Giant roly-polies, huh? I think we've been to your homeworld before." He turned towards the kitchen to yell, "Hey, Mama. Do you remember fighting a bunch of roly-polies?"

"Oh, yeah," she said, thinking back. "That was before we were even dating. It was to repair a wall or something."

Cupcake's boney jaw dropped. "You guys were

there for that?" he asked. "My mom said the Federation wouldn't send help. She said our world would be dead if it wasn't for a few squads that ignored them."

Mama set a plate of hotdogs down on the table. "The Senate didn't want to *waste resources* on a human homeworld," she explained. "About a dozen squads went anyway. Ours was one of them."

"It got pretty rough," Dada said, putting food on Ana's plate. He turned to Mama. "Remember that big one? I probably used fifty grenades before it finally went down."

"Remember that one I sliced open? Its guts exploded all over you?" Mama laughed. "I thought you were going to cry!"

"I wasn't crying," Dada protested. "It smelled so bad, and it burned my eyes."

Everyone laughed, but the children suddenly saw their parents differently.

"That's so cool," Wilber said in awe. Still, he couldn't believe it. How could this man—the guy who played video games in his underwear—be a grenade-throwing hero? And the woman who limited his candy intake, could she really have sliced up monsters?

"I can't wait to tell my mom I met you," Cupcake

said, putting mustard on his hotdog. "She's going to be so impressed. Did you know my people celebrate that as a holiday? We call it Rebuilder's Week. If it weren't for what you did, I probably wouldn't even be born. And the federation didn't even give you anything for all the trouble you went through."

Mama gave Cupcake a side hug. "I'm just glad we could help. That's what Christians do."

As they ate, they laughed and told stories. Dada repeatedly told jokes that made the children roll their eyes. Mama only had to ask Wilber to eat his vegetables once. Cupcake repeatedly thanked them for inviting him. Once the meal was finished, everyone helped clean the table.

Dada leaned against the kitchen counter while putting the dishes in the top rack of the dishwasher. "I know you guys are excited to start adventuring, but Mama and I think you should call it a day."

"Not fair," Wilber said. Ana stuck out her tongue.

Mama gave them a stern look. "Be respectful," she advised. "We thought maybe Cupcake could stay the night."

"Really?" Edith asked, excited.

"If it's okay with his parents," Mama said. She

turned to Cupcake. "Do you have a way of asking?"

Cupcake nodded. He pulled a glass orb from his apron pockets. "This bauble will take her a message and bring one back. It needs a couple hours to get back and forth, but it works alright."

"That's great," Mama said, turning to her own children. "We should get one of those."

"I'll go record a message and send it," Cupcake said.

"But what if someone sees him?" Wilber asked.

"It's okay," Dada assured them. "The same stuff that keeps us protected from Babylon will make him look invisible."

Cupcake nodded. He left the kitchen and went onto the back deck. He closed the glass door behind him, but the family could still see him talking into the orb.

"Dada," Wilber growled. "Why won't you let us go back? We have to find Sushi. Babylon is coming."

Dada knelt down, so they were face to face. "There will always be a danger. If you push yourself too hard, you'll get exhausted. It's a marathon, not a sprint."

Wilber pounded his fist on the table. "I don't either know what that means. I never know what that means."

Mama put her arm around him. "It means you need to take breaks and rest sometimes. Besides, Dada and I want to learn more about Cupcake."

"If you guys are going to spend time together," Dada explained. "We want to make sure he is a good guy."

"Why are you judging him," Edith asked. "He's our friend."

"I know, dear, but sometimes it's more complicated than that," Mama explained. "When I first started adventuring, I joined up with a pixie named Dingle. She said she was my friend, but she was lying. She stole all my gear and left me alone in a haunted castle. I almost didn't make it out."

"That does sound scary," Edith admitted.

"We know a few things about adventuring and squads—some of it we learned the hard way," Dada explained. "If you want to have friends, we have to approve. Dingle was a spy for Babylon, and we didn't know until it was too late."

The children nodded. "Okay," Edith agreed.

"I'm not going to trust anyone ever," Wilber said, puffing his chest with pride.

"That's not exactly what we're saying," Dada cautioned. "That's as bad as trusting the wrong people."

Wilber shrugged.

Cupcake finished speaking and threw the orb into

the sky. It shot from his hand like a rocket, ripping through clouds.

"Now we have to wait for it to come back," Cupcake said, walking back into the house.

Mama came upstairs with a couple board games. "Well, how about we play one of these until it does."

When they finished their first board game, the orb fell towards the house like a comet. It stopped before crashing into the back door. Gently, it knocked against the wooden frame. Mama opened the door, and the orb flew into Cupcake's hands.

A shrill, angry voice exited the orb. "You know I don't care where you stay," the woman said. "Stop bugging me."

Cupcake slowly put the orb back in his apron. He didn't look anyone in the eyes, and the room was quiet.

"Don't worry about it," Dada said, putting his hand on Cupcake's shoulder. "We're glad you can stay."

"Yeah," Wilber said.

Dada clapped his hands together. "Let's play a few more games, we'll order a pizza for dinner, and we can make root beer floats for dessert."

The next day, the squad woke up early, and Mama made them breakfast. Wilber snuck the powdered sugar and sprinkled some on his eggs. Rebel stole pieces of sausage that fell on the floor, and Edith helped feed Ana.

Cupcake sat down. "My friend at the docks sent me an orb this morning. I just got it," Cupcake explained. "He said Sushi's back on Ned."

"Goodie!" Edith shouted.

"But there's bad news," Cupcake explained. "She just signed up to fight in the Arena. If we want to find her before she leaves again, that's where we have to go."

The parents and Cupcake shared a knowing glance.

"The Arena is a pretty mean place," Mama said. "Do you hang out there often?"

Cupcake shook his head nervously, and his skull rattled as he did. "I hate it there," he admitted. "Only bullies go to the Arena."

Dada nodded. "Are you ready to go to a place like that?" he asked his children.

Wilber rolled his eyes, and Edith did a half-shrug.

"Sushi's the only one that knows what Babylon is doing on Earth," Edith said, partly to herself. She thought for a while longer and then turned to her parents. "If we want her help, I think we have to go to the Arena."

Wilber nodded. "I fink so too. What do you guys fink?"

Mama took a deep breath. "I agree," she eventually said. "But I want you to understand... this will be the hardest thing you've ever had to do. You might get beat up, and you'll probably get hurt feelings. Are you prepared for that?"

Everyone but Cupcake nodded.

"I'm not," Cupcake admitted. "But I'll go for you guys."

After breakfast, they followed their rings to the nearest park. Dada gave Cupcake a hoodie, so no one would get scared seeing a living skeleton. This time, the portal was between the 4th and 5th rungs of the monkey bars. It was only noticeable from the top, and falling through was easy.

When they got to Uncle Ned, they hitched a ride on a crab. It hurried along until she came across an open hole. To the surprise of the children, she jumped in. Quickly, the crab crawled deep underground. It was completely dark except for a few lanterns. Small candles hung on heavy wooden beams, and rail carts laid scattered in corners and at dead ends.

"Where are we going?" Edith asked, a little nervous.

"I don't like the dark either," Cupcake admitted. "But the Arena is under Ned's belly."

This trip was longer than the other crab rides they had experienced. Inside the dirt on Ned's back was a winding maze of mines and volcanic cracks. Wilber noticed both sisters getting scared, so he invited them to play 20 Questions. Cupcake said his Earth didn't have that game, so they taught him the rules.

Eventually, the crab crawled out of a hole and emerged outside a giant stadium. It hung from under Uncle Ned and spread out like a rocky cove. The place was packed. There were over ten thousand creatures in the stands. The children couldn't see them all from outside, but they could hear them cheer whenever something happened on the field.

"So cool," Wilber said.

Bridges and catwalks stretched to dangling spires of stone. Beneath them were the infinite spaces in which the giant crab stood.

"This is the PvP Arena," Cupcake explained. "People can fight other people here without permanently hurting each other."

Edith looked puzzled. "What does that mean?"

"It means you can die and get hurt, but after the fight, everything goes back to normal. I don't fully understand how." Cupcake moved his hands as if casting a magic spell. "It's science."

They entered the stadium and walked through the crowds. Once inside, they could see a giant bear on the field. It was the size of their house, and a battalion of soldiers tried to take it down. The bear charged the fighters, sending a few people flying. Even the helicopters were no match. The bear just stood up on its back legs and swatted them out of the air. The crowd cheered wildly as dozens of men and women rolled on the ground in pain.

Edith was stunned, if not disgusted. "Mama and Dada were right; this place is *not* appropriate."

Cupcake led them past the betting station to the Fighter's Pit.

"All the fighters wait here before taking the field," Cupcake explained. "If we want to talk to Sushi, we have to go in there."

"Wait," Wilber said. His eyes were wide. "Sushi's going to fight that bear?"

Cupcake nodded. "It's the Titan Bash," he said

nervously. "It's one of the most popular events on Ned. People fight young Titans until one is defeated. A few years ago, it lasted a month before someone finally defeated one of the titans."

Edith watched the bear swallow a soldier whole. She knew it was all pretend—and that the soldiers would be better after the fight—but her hands were still shaking.

"I don't feel like getting any closer to the field," she said, trembling.

Wilber nodded, "But if we want to find out how Babylon plans to take over Earth, we have to."

Ana pointed forward, and Rebel barked.

As they entered the fighter pit, they saw Sushi sitting by the door to the field. She was the same beautiful mermaid, but she looked different.

Sushi was no longer the sweet and innocent mermaid they saw in the seashell. She now wore an eyepatch over her left eye and was covered in tattoos, piercings, and scars. But that wasn't the most surprising change.

"What happened to her tail?" Wilber asked.

"Merfolk have a special ability called 'Leg Up,'" Cupcake explained. "As long as they stay hydrated, they can take human form. The trouble is, the longer they stay human, the harder it is to stay hydrated."

"Do you think she'll even remember us?" Edith asked. "She was almost dead when we met her."

Wilber shrugged.

They walked across the fighter pit and stood in front of Sushi. Her eyes were down, focused on the giant anchor she used as a weapon. She was sharpening it with a black seashell.

"Do you remember us?" Edith asked shyly.

Sushi looked up, annoyed. However, when she saw the children, her expression softened. She nodded.

Edith rocked on her feet nervously. "We wondered if you would help us save our planet."

Sushi frowned.

Wilber fidgeted with his hands. "Well, you see, umm... Remember... you said Babylon had spies living on our planet. You said they would eventually break our home. Remember?"

"I remember," she said.

"Right," Edith nodded. "So, will you help us?"

Sushi rubbed her temples and sighed loudly. "I do hate Orcs," she mumbled to herself.

"So you'll join us?" Edith asked, clapping her hands.

Ana clapped, copying her big sister.

"I didn't say that," Sushi snapped. "You guys don't look very strong, and I don't want to waste my time with a bunch of babies."

"We won't waste your time," Edith promised.

Wilber flexed his muscles. "We're strong, too."

Sushi held up her hands. "Stop talking," she growled. "If you fight with me in the Arena—and if you aren't horrible—I'll join your squad."

The kids looked at the Bear, back to Sushi, and then at each other.

Edith tried to think through all their options. She turned around and spoke only to Wilber and Ana. "We haven't even used our weapons once. Do you think it's worth trying?"

Ana repositioned herself on Rebel's saddle. She took a deep breath, smacked her fist against her chest, and roared. "Me. Fight. You. Fight," she said, pointing to her siblings.

"Okay, Ana," Wilber agreed, getting pumped. "Let's do it."

Wilber then turned to Cupcake. He put his arm around the skeleton and whispered, "You with us?"

"I'm your mentor," Cupcake finally admitted. "I

have to be."

Wilber nodded. He spun around and clapped his hands. "Let's do this fing!" he shouted. "Us versus a Titan. Let's go!"

TITAN BASH

After the Bear destroyed or ate all the soldiers, a blue laser moved horizontally across the field. Every person the light touched was restored to full health.

"That light removes the arena spell," Cupcake explained. "The magic makes it seem like everything is real, but the light turns it off and makes things go back to normal."

The Bear roared loudly. It stood in the middle of the arena while confetti fell from the sky. The crowd cheered, celebrating the titan's victory. As that happened, the soldiers exited the field. The guy eaten by the bear walked past Edith. "That was the worst," he said. "No way that was worth the XP or loot."

Edith began to fidget. She turned to her brother. "Uh, are we sure we want to do this?"

"Too late now," Sushi said with a smirk.

A Dittomark robot entered the room where they were waiting. He had the same gold body, but he wore a military uniform. There was a nametag stitched on his shirt that read, "Sgt. Grump."

"Listen up, you puke-filled little barf bags," Grump said. "The better the show, the better rewards at the end. If you die easy, this will hardly be worth the pain."

"Pain?!" Wilber asked. "I thought it was for pretend."

Sergeant Grump laughed. "Little baby, you're going to feel everything. It'll go away at the end of the fight, but until then, the pain is real."

"Meh," Ana said, gripping her sword with one hand and the pommel of Rebel's saddle with the other.

"So here's the deal," Grump said. "The announcer will call your names, and that's when you'll go into the ring. Once everyone is in, they'll bring in the next Titan."

Edith looked around the room. "Are we the only ones fighting?" she asked.

Grump got in Edith's face so that they were nearly touching. "Are you feeling lonely, little girl?" he asked mockingly. "Do you want your Mama to come give you a little kiss?"

Edith nodded a little.

"I'll take one too," Wilber joked.

Ana raised her hand. "Me!"

Grump screamed. "I was making fun, you idiots!" He shook his head. "Another squad is scheduled to fight this round, but for some reason, they got approved to sign up anonymously. Now get in line."

The children, Cupcake, and Sushi all lined up. Rebel scratched his ear with his leg, jiggling Ana's saddle and making her laugh.

A loud voice boomed over the arena intercom. "Welcome to the 11th day of Titan Bash," the announcer said over the loudspeakers. Everyone cheered wildly. "For the last hundred years, we've been doing Titan Bash, but we've never had a Titan as big as our next contestant."

"Oh, great," Cupcake muttered.

"Will this be the round that ends the celebration?" the announcer asked. The crowd cheered wildly again. "From the looks of the roster, it doesn't look like it."

Everyone laughed.

"Well, that's rude," Edith said.

"Should we meet our competitors?" the announcer asked the stadium. "First up, we have Sushi. She's a pirate from the now-destroyed homeworld: Moon Mermoni. Sushi's the only known survivor. So sad. Give her some love."

Sushi left the pit and entered the field. The crowd clapped respectfully.

"Next up, we have a cursed alchemist named Cupcake. He's an ugly-looking dude, but let's give it up for him anyway."

The crowd laughed as Cupcake entered the field.

"Why are they being so mean?" Edith asked.

"I don't know," Wilber answered. He then cupped his hands around his mouth. "Don't listen to them, Cupcake. You got this."

The announcer spoke again. "And next up, we have a squad of humans." Everyone laughed. "What's worse, I heard they are... *Christians*."

The mood of ten thousand people shifted. Laughter turned to boos and angry yells. "That's right, people. We have a Barbarian, Wizard, Heavy Gunner, and their Familiar. These losers have zero XP and almost no street cred."

The children froze.

"Move it," Grump said, pushing them forward. "Your turn to get out there."

As the kids entered, they could feel the anger—the hatred.

"How about this, folks," the announcer said. "Place your bets now. If you can guess which cries first, you'll win a free lemon-berry slushie at the concession stand."

The crowd laughed.

"Well, you might think this will be a disappointing match," the announcer said. "You might think this will be a waste of your time. But have we ever given you a bad show? Of course not."

The lights in the arena dimmed. The sound cut out, and the crowd was hushed. A faint sound began to play over the speakers. As the anticipation built, so did the music. Suddenly, lights danced around the arena. The music boomed dramatically, and a squad appeared in the air.

They fell from under Uncle Ned, and as the dust settled, an orc and four other people appeared in the center of the field. The crowd went nuts. Ana shrunk a little, covering her ears from the sound. The children were surprised to find Cupcake cheering, and even Sushi had a slight smile on her face.

"This is the most decorated group of adventurers in all the infinite worlds," the announcer described. "They have the highest scores in the PvP Arena, and second's not even close. There's no one you'd rather be, and there's no one we love more."

With every word, the cheers grew louder. The whole world under Uncle Ned shook. "That's right, everyone, Razorface and his squad is joining the fight!"

Cupcake turned to the kids. "This is great news for us," he explained, no longer nervous. "Even though rewards are based on your contribution to the fight, everyone gets a bonus if you win."

"Aren't orcs bad guys, though?" Wilber asked.

"Most are," he answered. "But there are a few good ones. Still, I wouldn't make one mad, even if they are good."

An arena employee ran out onto the field. He held a microphone up to the orc. The crowd was chanting, "Ra-zor-face! Ra-zor-face!"

Wilber leaned closer to Cupcake. He had to shout to be heard over the crowd. "Is this guy really that cool?"

Cupcake nodded.

"Been a long time," the orc said, spitting on the microphone as he talked. "And we brought a new fighter. This is Ninja Desh." When Razorface was done with the introduction, he ate the microphone.

"Alright, everyone," the announcer spoke again. "Razorface made a special request to the Lord of Dragons for his best fighter... and the next titan should be arriving any moment now."

That's when they heard it. The sound of a dozen tornadoes. Hovering over the stadium—but still under the rocky belly of Uncle Ned—was the most enormous dragon. Every beat of the dragon's wings sent a gust of wind through the stadium. One guy was even blown out of his seat. An arena employee with a jet pack had to rescue him before he floated off into space.

The beast landed on the ground with a tremendous thud.

"This is the most powerful creature we have ever had in the arena, and Razorface brought it for your viewing enjoyment," the announcer said. "I don't know about you all, but I can't wait to see how well Razorface, Lady Dumptruck, Crowbar, Chad, and Desh can do against such a powerful beast."

The crowd was going bonkers. Creatures were

shaking each other, some were fainting, and someone was constantly shouting, "We love you, Razorface!"

"Well," Wilber said. "I think we better pray."

Ana nodded.

The three knelt down and bowed their heads. So did Rebel. As they were about to talk to God, the crowd busted into laughter again.

Wilber looked up and saw everyone in the audience pointing and laughing at them. He turned to Cupcake. "Don't they believe in God?" he asked.

Cupcake was reluctant to speak. His skull wouldn't look the children in the eyes. "They believe in a lot of gods. Just not yours."

Wilber turned back to his siblings. He started to panic. "They're making me feel embarrassed."

Edith put her arm around her siblings. "It's okay," she comforted. "Let's ask God for help."

Wilber nodded. "Dear God," he prayed. "Please keep us safe, and help Sushi want to join our squad. Please don't let us get hurt. But most importantly, help these people see that you love them and that you're powerful."

"Amen," the three said at the same time.

CHAPTER 13
HALF AND HALF

Immediately after the children finished praying, a loud gong rang out across the Arena. The dragon roared, and four more heads sprouted from its massive body. Fire spewed from three of the heads, and the other two chomped viciously.

"Oh no," Cupcake said, "It's a hydragon."

"What's a hydragon?" Wilber questioned loudly.

"Half hydra. Half dragon," Cupcake explained. "The heads can't instantly regenerate, but they're all dragon strong. I've never seen one in real life."

The children didn't know what to do. They were

paralyzed with fear. All they could do was stand, mouths agape. Rebel whimpered and tried to hide behind Wilber, taking Ana with him.

"No. No, Rebi," Ana shouted, trying to steer the puppy into battle.

Razorface and his squad flew over the kids with one mighty leap. Everyone moved so fast that the children could barely process what was happening.

Desh continuously appeared and disappeared all around the arena. Each time he revealed his location, ninja stars exploded from his position. After a few attacks, he eventually hit the hydragon in the eyes, blinding one of the five heads.

The crowd cheered wildly.

Lady Dumptruck seized the opportunity. She was an orange construction robot and jumped into the hydragon's blind spot. With an enormous thud, she landed beside the hydragon's legs. One of the heads spewed fire at her, but she shielded herself with a snowplow.

In addition to the snowplow, Lady Dumptruck came equipped with a wrecking ball. She swung it above her head, and fire bounced off her shield. As the wrecking ball gained momentum, she let loose of the chain, and the ball crashed into the hydragon's face. Giant fangs broke out of its mouth and landed on the ground by Wilber.

"They're the size of footballs," Wilber murmured.

With one of the heads blinded and dazed, Razorface jumped in. He swung his broad sword so mightily that thunder echoed through the stadium. The blade sliced through the hydragon's skin, cutting one of the heads from its body.

The audience went ballistic. Even the announcer cheered. "Un-be-lievable," he said. "One head down, four more to go."

Still, the children were frozen with fear. Even without one of its heads, the hydragon was winning. Fire billowed and belched from the colossal beast, burning everything around them. It swung its long tail, hitting Chad in the gut. There was so much force behind the blow the zombie went flying across the stadium.

"Move it," Sushi said, charging past the stunned kids.

She moved her hands, and streams of water shot from her fingers. With the rhythmic movements, she put out fires as fast as the hydragon could make them. It was like a beautiful dance.

"Right," Cupcake said. He pulled a stone bowl and a whisk from his apron. With rapid-fast moments, he added ingredients and started stirring. "I'll start making some healing potions and buffs."

The hydragon snarled and snapped at Razorface. Although the orc tried to dodge, hydragon's teeth tore through his armor. Even the incredibly brave and famous Razorface yelled out in pain.

Wilber's gun felt a little heavier in his hands. "Uhhhh, I fink maybe we are gonna need more prayer."

Edith clenched her teeth in anger. "They were laughing at *God*," she said, stressing the words. She tightened her hands around the wizard's staff and aimed it at the hydragon.

Ana nodded. She clicked her heels into Rebel's side, and the puppy moved in front of her siblings. She pulled her sword off her back and smacked it against the ground. The baby screamed so loud, the screeching hurt even her own ears.

Wilber lifted his gun and took a deep breath. "You're right," he said. "Let's do this!"

"One second," Cupcake said. He threw a bird eyeball into something that looked like cake batter. After stirring, he scooped some up and rolled it in his boney palms. Eventually, he had a little cake ball. "This will improve your aim."

Cautiously, Wilber grabbed the cake bite and tossed it in his mouth. With the first chew, he could feel his eyesight improve. Suddenly, he could see everything better. The hydragon was now visible in complete detail. He could see every scale, fin, and fang on the hydragon.

"Awesome," Wilber shouted, lifting his rifle. "I'm gonna snipe this fool."

Wilber pulled the trigger, and a large burst of laser shot from the gun. The force kicked so hard that Wilber flew back and fell to the ground. The laser wiggled through the sky, missing the hydragon and exploding against an invisible barrier that protected the audience.

"Poop in a shoe," Wilber said. He massaged the place the rifle kicked his shoulder. "That really hurt."

Cupcake knelt down and put salve on Wilber's shoulder. Instantly, Wilber stopped whining. He got up, dusted himself off, and lifted his gun.

"Wow," Wilber said. "Thanks!"

"Don't mention it," Cupcake said, already working on a different potion. "But you might want to be more careful. I can't waste ingredients every time you shoot your gun."

Razorface, his squad, and Sushi were still fighting the hydragon while the children learned how to use their weapons. Even though the other fighters attacked with powerful booming blows, the hydragon barely took any damage.

"Aright, Edith. Your turn," Wilber said. "You can't do any worse than I did."

Edith lifted her staff and pointed it at the hydragon. She waited. Nothing happened.

"Is it broken?" Edith looked closely at the staff to see if there was an on/off switch or something. After a few seconds, she tried again. Still, nothing happened. "I don't know what I'm supposed to do," she finally admitted.

Cupcake looked up from his recipe book for a second. "You have to say a magic word. Usually, low-level wizards only have one spell. I think it's 'ice blast.' Try that."

Edith again held up her staff. She pointed at the hydragon, spoke clearly, and whispered, "Ice blast."

Frost formed around the end of the staff, but nothing happened. Edith looked at it angrily and stomped her foot. "I think it's broken."

Wilber patted her on the shoulder. "It's okay. You'll get it," he comforted. "Try yelling it."

Edith nodded and stepped toward the hydragon. She took a deep breath, lifted the staff, and yelled, "ICE! BLAST!"

The staff shook as an icicle shot from the end of the staff. It flew across the arena, leaving a trail of snow where it went. The kids watched it fly toward the hydragon, but Edith had been so focused on getting it to work that she forgot to aim.

The icicle hit Razorface in the shoulder, exploding across his armor.

"Oooh, Sorry," Edith said, covering her mouth with her hand. "Sorry. Sorry. Sorry."

Razorface turned around, annoyed. He scowled at her and then turned back to the fight.

"Well," Wilber said. "Ana and Rebel, you're up next. Let's see what you got."

Rebel took a few steps forward. Ana was sitting securely on the saddle. She lifted her sword, balanced it awkwardly in the air, and pointed forward. Rebel used his dash collar to sprint across the arena. As the puppy moved by the hydragon, Ana used her strength belt to swing her sword. The blade bounced off the hydragon's tough hide, doing no damage.

Still dashing, Rebel was back by the other children in the blink of an eye.

"Well," Wilber said, "we're pretty much the worst."

Over the next hour, the kids continued to practice their new skills while trying to stay as far away from the hydragon as possible. With each shot, spell, and swing, they learned a little more about how to fight. At one point, Ana even did enough damage to take 1 HP off the hydragon.

Periodically, while the children practiced, Razorface and his squad would incapacitate another head: Zombie Chad chewed through one of the necks, actually turning one of the heads into a zombie that fought against its own body; Lady Dumptruck plowed through a third head, knocking it unconscious; and Crowbar, the human-sized opossum, broke the fourth neck by continually hitting it with a tire iron.

Only one head was left, and Ninja Desh had already hit it with a dozen smoke bombs. The hydragon was confused and angry, burping fire everywhere.

Wilber was panting. "I don't think he's ever going to die."

Ana slid out of her saddle and plopped down on the

ground. She folded her arms and began to cry.

Wilber fell down. "Just have the hydragon stomp my head," he shouted. "I give up."

"We can do this," Edith encouraged. She surveyed the battle. The hydragon seemed more powerful than ever, even after losing 3 heads and one fighting against itself. The beast moved so violently that no one could get close—not even Razorface.

"Guys, we can't give up," Edith pleaded.

Wilber rolled onto his back. "I tried my hardest, and I couldn't even hurt him."

Edith's lower lip quivered. She, too, felt like giving up. "If we don't do a good job, Sushi won't join us," she reminded her siblings. "And if Sushi doesn't join us, we'll never find the spies. And if we don't find the spies, Babylon will take over Earth."

No one said anything for a few moments.

"Okay, gurl," Wilber said, slowly pulling himself off the ground. He held his rifle with both hands. "What's the plan."

Edith thought for a moment. "Well, if we can't hurt him, what can we do?"

Wilber shrugged. "Pray someone else can?"

"Yeah. I have an idea!" Edith shouted. "What if we

distracted the hydragon by praying. Everyone in the arena hates it when we do that, and maybe the hydragon does too. If we can cause a big enough distraction, the other fighters can finish him off."

Wilber scratched his shoulder as he thought. The weight of the gun strap was giving him a rash. "Alright," he agreed. "I like it."

Ana folded her hands and tilted her head to the side. "Pray," she agreed.

Her siblings joined her, folding their hands and bowing their heads. Even Rebel looked down and crossed his paws.

"Dear God," Wilber shouted. "We love you, and we don't care what anyone finks."

Laughter filled the stadium. "Here we go again," the announcer said. "The babies are praying for a second time. Let's see if their god can save them. And for those not paying attention, the Barbarian cried first. If anyone guessed that, you get a free slushie at the concession stand."

Edith clenched her jaw in anger. "God, help us forgive people who make fun of us. Help us to love them like you love them."

The hydragon emerged from the smoke cloud. As it

did, its eyes were locked on the children. Hatred made the stadium shake. They didn't know if the hydragon was against God or if the beast saw four easy kills. Either way, the hydragon was enraged. Fire blew everywhere as it charged the children and puppy.

"Jee-jush," Ana said, "Pray. Me. Eda. Wihl.'"

The hydragon stretched its long neck for the children. Within seconds, the beast would be on top of them, but the other fighters saw what was happening. The hydragon was totally unprotected and open for attack.

Cupcake tossed the last of his potions and buffs to the other fighters. They quickly ate bakery items and drank juice boxes until they were all back to full strength... then they made their move. Sushi, Razorface, Desh, Lady Dumptruck, Crowbar, and Chad—they all attacked. They dropped like a nuke and destroyed the hydragon's last head with one unified blow.

But the hydragon was moving too fast, and it was too close to the children. Its enormous body died, and it collapsed on the children, crushing them all.

CHAPTER

14

CHURCH SERMON

The blue light moved horizontally across the arena. Everything the light touched returned to normal. Cupcake's inventory was returned, and all the other fighters had their armor and health restored. The children and Rebel were also brought back to life.

Edith gasped as she woke up. "It felt like we died," she screamed. She wrapped her arms around Ana, who was also crying.

Wilber hugged Rebel. "That was super scary."

"What an incredible finish to the Titan Bash," the announcer cheered. "As we figured, the humans were completely worthless… But Razorface and his squad did not disappoint."

The fans cheered so loudly that the stadium was again shaking.

Razorface walked across the field to where the hydragon stood. All five heads, now restored, merged back into the one giant dragon head.

"Good game," Razorface said, raising his fist to the dragon.

The dragon gave Razorface a fist bump. "You too," the beast said. His voice was young, high-pitched, and squeaky.

Again, the announcer spoke, but it was hard to hear him over the roar of the crowd. "If you're looking for a souvenir from this year's Titan Bash, we just had some t-shirts made. They say, 'The best part of Titan Bash 5103' above a picture of those crying human babies. They're super hilarious and only cost 10 creds."

The children were tired, scared, and embarrassed. They quickly got up and ran to Cupcake.

"Can you get us out of here?" Wilber asked.

Cupcake nodded and called a crab. Sushi followed, and when the crab got there, everyone got on. The children sat close to each other, and Rebel whined softly at their feet. Their skin was pale, and they couldn't speak.

The crab carried them off Ned. They went through portals, across different dimensions, and through time. It was a long journey, and yet no one said a thing.

Eventually, Cupcake leaned forward. "Just keep reminding yourself that it wasn't real."

"That was the *worst*," Wilber said, throwing up his hands. "We shouldn't have gone there. That was super scary... and everyone made fun of us... and it was a waste of time."

"Not a waste," Sushi said. "We won because of you."

Wilber looked up a little encouraged.

"Even Razorface was about to give up," she continued.

Cupcake smiled with a big toothy grin. "So, you'll help them? Join their squad?"

"I don't know how we'll pull it off," Sushi explained as the crab landed in the children's backyard. "But I'll help you find the spies on your world."

The children unloaded and walked inside with Rebel behind them. When they saw Mama, they instantly started crying. They told her everything—how they pretend-died and how everyone made fun of them.

Mama held her children and comforted them the best she could, but the children couldn't stop crying.

"We prayed to God, and He didn't help," Edith cried. "Why didn't He make us strong?"

That night was filled with nightmares and sleeplessness. Even Rebel howled in the backyard. Eventually, Dada gathered all the children into the parents' bed. Finally, they all fell asleep while Rebel snored at the foot of the bed.

The next day, the children sat around the breakfast table.

Edith spoke firmly. "I'm not going back."

"Me either," Wilber agreed.

Ana nodded. "Me. No go'n."

"We couldn't even do any damage to that dragon," Wilber shouted, not realizing he was getting louder the longer he talked. "If we can only do zero damage... that's like... *zero* damage... then Babylon will destroy us. Like, totally destroy us."

Mama helped the children put jelly on their biscuits. "You know, when we first started talking about this, I didn't want you to go. I was afraid something like this would happen," Mama explained, fighting back the tears. "The thought of this broke my heart."

Wilber slumped in his chair. Edith leaned forward and put her head in her arms. Ana covered her eyes with her hands.

"But I was wrong," she admitted. "If Babylon takes over Earth, the whole world will wake up feeling like you do now."

Dada nodded. "I wish our future was easier, but God's calling us to live a different life."

Mama took a deep breath and composed herself. "We can't protect you from all the bad things that are coming, but we can teach you how to have faith when they do."

"Please don't make us go back," Edith begged. "We just want to stay with you."

Wilber shook Dada's arm. "They're all too strong. Don't make us go back."

Mama went to say something, but Dada stopped her. "Let's take a break from talking about this," he said. "We have church today, so let's just focus on that."

The children tried to protest, but Dada silenced them with a stern look.

The ride to church was quiet. Mama and Dada tried

to engage the children with fun music and jokes, but not even Ana was interested.

When they got to church, the children went to Sunday school while Mama and Dada served in another classroom. During the second hour, the family all went to church together.

Mama and Dada brought coloring books and toys, but the children didn't feel like playing. They just sat in their seats, staring blankly at the stage.

"We know Jesus is about to face some dark times," preached a man from the stage. "His friends are about to betray him. The people he came to save are about to kill him. So what do you think he tells his friends the night before all that happens?"

The children imagined Jesus probably felt the same way they did. Wilber expected Jesus to be mad at the people who made fun of him. Edith guessed Jesus would be angry at God for not protecting him. Ana imagined Jesus was sad because no one was there to hug him.

"We don't have to imagine because John chapter 16 tells us," the pastor continued. "Jesus told his friend that even though things are about to get really... really... bad... things will eventually get really... really... good."

The children felt themselves being pulled in. Their

breathing grew deep, and they hung on every word.

"All these bad things were about to happen. And yet Jesus only cared about one thing: comforting his friends," the pastor taught. "Jesus told his disciples to have peace. Why? Because Jesus knows how the story ends. Death and Satan might look strong now, but their power is fading. In the end, God wins. Doesn't that give you hope? Doesn't that give you joy?"

Dada reached over and grabbed Edith's hand. She took hold of Wilber's, Wilber held Ana's, and Ana held Mama's. The entire family held hands and looked at each other. They were all thinking the same thing.

"God's talking to us," Edith whispered.

Wilber nodded enthusiastically.

"Me," Ana shouted loud enough to distract the other families around her.

"Jesus doesn't say they should have joy because life is easy. In fact, he says life will be the opposite. Bad things will happen. Hard things will break your heart. You will feel alone," the pastor said. "But you will not be alone. Do you know why? Because God is with you. And the bad things cannot beat you because Jesus has beaten death."

Both the parents and children had tears in their

eyes. Not tears born from pain, fear of death, or embarrassment. No. This time, they cried tears of joy and peace.

"I don't know what you're facing today," the pastor said. "But Jesus lived this life, and he conquered it all, even death. If you have given your life to Jesus, then what do you have to fear? The son of God and all his power lives inside you. So when God calls you to do something big, act like He's there helping you. Because He is!"

After church, the family left the building celebrating over what they had heard.

"I'm ready to go back to Uncle Ned," Wilber screamed.

"Me too," Edith agreed. "I'm still scared we're going to keep getting hurt, but I believe God will win in the end."

Ana raised her hand. "Me," she screamed.

Dada opened the van door and let everyone in. "If you guys are serious about going back," he said, "then invite your friends over. We have a lot of planning to do."

CHAPTER

15

NEW COMMAND POST

Mama and Dada gathered everyone into the homework room, even Cupcake and Sushi. It had a giant corkboard on the wall, desks for drawing or writing, bean bags for reading, and cabinets filled with art supplies. Everyone sat down, and Sushi shared what she knew.

"During the evacuation, I intercepted a transmission from Babylon," Sushi told the parents. "The message was garbled, but we traced the signal here."

Mama refilled everyone's lemonade. "Babylon has

always had spies on Earth—they do everywhere. What makes you think they're going to invade?"

"After we lost our war, not many of us were left. We had to be strategic about where we hit back." Sushi made a punching movement with her hand. Ana mimicked the gesture. "We'd never heard of your homeworld, so we guessed there'd only be a small orc base here—one we could easily take out."

Dada leaned back. "I feel like there's a big 'but' coming."

Wilber laughed. "Big butt."

Sushi didn't laugh. "When we got to your solar system, an Orc Battlecruiser was waiting for us. They attacked, and I was shot down. That's when my shell crashed in your neighbor's backyard."

Wilber's eyes grew wide. He swung his hands wildly as he spoke. "We saw that battle on the screens in your shell. It was out by that big planet with the red dot. I forget what it's called," he informed his parents.

"Oh, yeah," Edith remembered. "There was a bunch of little ships fighting that one ginormous garbage one."

"They won't invade with just one ship," Dada said, creating a mental timeline. He left the room and came back with his trunk.

"They'll probably need a few cruisers to take over a planet like ours," Mama said, helping Dada open the trunk.

Wilber's jaw dropped. "Our planet must be powerful."

Sushi shook her head. "Not really. They needed over a hundred to take Mermoni, and my planet's just a moon."

Dada pulled out a little UFO from his trunk. It was a silver disc with a green dome. When he pushed the top, two digital eyes and a mouth appeared.

A robotic voice emanated from the screen. "How can Foh be of service?" it asked.

"Foh, I need you to go to Jupiter. Babylon is staging an invasion force, and we need to know how many ships are there. You need to go and report back," Dada ordered. "Do you understand?"

"Foh copies," the little UFO repeated.

Foh struggled to fly off Dada's hand but eventually took to the air. It slowly dawdled across the room, sputtering exhaust like an old car. Mama rolled her eyes as it crashed into the closed window.

"Error. Error. Error," Foh said as it fell to the floor. "Foh has been shot."

"No, you haven't," Mama said, annoyed. She opened the window, picked up Foh, and threw it out the window. "I don't know why you keep using that thing."

"I love Foh," Dada protested. "He cracks me up."

"Over and out," Foh said, jetting upwards after bumping into the neighbor's house.

"So... that was weird," Wilber said.

Sushi shook her head. "Anyway, Babylon won't invade a world unless their spies tell them how and when to do it."

Cupcake spoke for the first time. "But how do we find the spies?"

"Remember how I said we intercepted a transmission? Well, I was thinking, if you can help me free my homeworld, we can use their communication device to find the spies on your world."

Once Sushi finished speaking, Mama and Dada looked at each other.

Edith tried to recap what she'd heard. "So, if we help you save your planet, we'll learn where the spies are on Earth, and you'll help us save our planet. Right?"

"Seems like a good plan," Dada eventually said. "What do you need?"

"Just a squad," Sushi said.

Mama tucked her hair behind her ears. "What about your ship?"

Sushi smiled a little. "That's why I needed to fight in the arena. I didn't have enough street cred to fix it on my own. But it should be fixed any minute now."

"Let's do this fing!" Wilber said, fist-pumping. In his excitement, he kicked over a small basket of crayons. Colors rolled across the room and covered the floor. Rebel ran over, lapping the crayons up like water.

Mama reached for the dog, grabbing him by the collar. "Wilber, pick them up before he gets rainbow diarrhea again."

Wilber obediently ran over and began fighting the puppy for whatever was still on the floor. After getting them in the box, he then pulled waxy crumbs from Rebel's mouth. Ana clapped at the commotion.

"Alright, alright," Dada said, calming everyone down with his hands. "While Wilber cleans that up, we have to do a couple of things. If you're going into battle together, you've got to decide where your loyalties are. Forming a squad means you fight for each other, protect each other, and listen to each other. Are you willing to do that?"

Everyone looked around the room, sizing each

other up. Ana shuffled to the middle of the room. She raised her hand as high as it could go. "Me," she said.

"Me too," Edith agreed, putting her hand on Ana's.

"Me three." As Wilber walked across the room, he tripped on the bucket of crayons, sending Rebel into another feeding frenzy. Mama just rubbed her temples, pretending to ignore the situation. "Sorry," he whispered, a big grimace on his face.

Cupcake put his hand in next. "You know what I'm going to say. I don't have a choice," he said. "But even if I wasn't your mentor, you guys are nice to me. I'll help you do anything."

Sushi was the last to put her hand in. "All my people are dead or captured. Everyone else is too afraid to help me," she admitted. "I'll take whatever I can get."

CHAPTER

16

UNDERSEA VOLCANO

The shell plummeted through the sky.

"Is this the best idea?" Edith asked.

The children were holding onto anything they could. Rebel whined as he slid across the floor of the spaceship.

Sushi didn't answer. Her entire body was pushed forward against the controls, causing the ship to fly even faster toward the planet. The speed and direction caused everyone to float out of their seats. Ana rolled through the air, giggling and laughing. Her giant sword banged loudly as she bounced from wall to wall.

"Weee," she giggled.

The shell hit the ocean hard, sending the squad back into their seats. Everyone screamed, and the collision rattled Cupcake's limbs from his body.

"That's embarrassing," he said, trying to reattach his wiggling arms and legs.

Wilber held his stomach and moaned. His face was green. "I fink I frew up in my mouth," he admitted. "And I swallowed it."

Once in the water, the shell moved at a safer pace. It swam through the moon's massive ocean and sunk deeper and deeper.

Rebel had ahold of Cupcake's arm. Edith chased him around the tiny shell. "Drop it!" she ordered. "Rebel, drop it. Bad dog."

Eventually, the children cornered the puppy and pulled the arm from his mouth. They then helped reattach it to Cupcake.

"Sorry," Edith said.

Sushi didn't speak. Her focus was on taking them deeper and deeper into the ocean. As they sank, Wilber looked outside one of the bubble windows.

"Where are all the fish?" he asked.

Sushi spoke bitterly. "The Orcs. They ruined

everything. Soon, my home will be just like the Deadlands."

"What are *deadlands*?" Wilber asked.

Cupcake trembled as he spoke. "Babylon makes some worlds sad, some worlds they make angry, and some they turn scary.

Sushi's voice was emotionless. "It means," she said, "what they don't kill, they eat or imprison."

Eventually, the ship reached the ocean depths. The light of the shell only illuminated a small area around them. There was nothing but an empty sandy floor covered by an endless black ocean. Sushi drove along until she found a rocky overhang.

"Perfect," she said, parking the shell underneath.

"Everyone ready?" Cupcake asked, handing out a handful of gummies.

Wilber stuck out his tongue. "What are these? They smell like fish guts!"

"I made them. They'll help you underwater."

Everyone ate some except for Sushi and Cupcake. Even Rebel had a handful.

Wilber put his hand on his stomach. "I fink I'm gonna puke."

"I don't feel good either," Edith said, covering her

mouth with her hand.

Cupcake patted them on the shoulder. "That means they're working."

Sushi put her hand on the door. "Ready?"

Everyone shook their head. "No!" Edith shouted. "We don't know how to swim underwater."

"Too late," Sushi shouted with a smirk. She flung the door open, letting gallons of deep sea ocean rush in. The inside flooded, and the children sloshed around the sides as if they were in the washing machine. Soon, there would be no air left for them to breathe, but something magical was happening.

"We're transforming," Wilber shouted over the sound of rushing water.

The second the water touched their skin, the gummies were activated in their body. Slowly, scales grew on their skin and spread down from their stomach. They also grew gills on their ribs and fins on their backs. Uncontrollably, their legs pulled together and merged into one big tail.

"I'm a mermaid," Edith shouted, doing a flip underwater.

"What about you?" Wilber asked Cupcake.

"You can't drown if you're mostly dead," he said, his

bones floating lifelessly underwater.

"Look at Rebel," Wilber laughed.

The dog swam around them like a little puppy-shark.

"Stop goofing off," Sushi ordered. "We only have three hours before you turn back into humans."

The squad followed Sushi out of the shell and into the ocean. The lights on the space shell disappeared in the distance. Soon, they found themselves alone in the pitch-black emptiness. They followed Sushi until they finally saw an underwater volcano on the horizon. Caves covered its sloping surface, and the glow of hot orange magma was the only light they could see.

"Careful," Wilber warned, pointing to the distance. "It's being guarded by a bunch of yucky monsters."

Edith swam to a nearby trench. "It looks like we could take this all the way to the volcano," she suggested. "They might not even see us."

Everyone nodded.

The trench was deep and just wide enough for them to swim through, one by one. Above their heads, they watched ghost-whales and zombie-sharks patrol the waters.

When they got to the base of the volcano, Sushi

made them wait. She pulled out a small piece of coral and spoke into the top. "Weapons: online. Autopilot: engage."

At first, nothing happened. Then, suddenly, all the spooky monsters darted away from the volcano.

The children peeked out of the trench only to find Sushi's ship rocketing towards them. Once close, it started freaking out. All by itself, the space shell flew through the ocean, zig-zagging, flipping, and doing barrel rolls. Not only that, but it opened fire. Tridents sliced through the water, and pearl bombs exploded everywhere. It was chaos.

A giant ghost whale hovered above them. "We need reinforcements," he groaned. "Send everyone."

Within minutes, a dozen undead sea creatures flooded out from the volcano caves. In addition to zombie sharks and ghost whales, there were also vampire eels, were-walruses, and a school of mummified tuna fish.

Wilber pumped his fist. "Good job, Sushi," he said. "There won't be anyone left inside."

The squad swam to the highest part of the volcano and looked in. Cages lined the interior walls. Lava gargled in the center, but a small flat rock floated on the surface. A dozen computers were on the rock, and the only one controlling them was a burly orc in a diver's suit.

"Look," Edith said, pointing to the cages. "There's hundreds of merfolk in there."

Sushi's eyes opened wide. "I don't believe it," she said, mostly to herself. "There is."

"Don't worry," Wilber said, putting his hand on her shoulders. "We'll free 'em all. We just have to beat up that boss guy."

Sushi grunted. "Cupcake, you stay up here. If any of the monsters start coming this way, let us know. Okay?"

Cupcake nodded. His boney body was trembling with fear.

"We got you," Wilber said. "Just call for help if you need us."

Edith looked at her waterproof kitty watch. "How much longer before the gummies wear off?"

"You only have one more hour," Cupcake said nervously.

Wilber nodded. He aimed his gun and waited for the signal to attack. Edith took a deep breath and began casting a spell. The end of her staff grew frosty, even underwater. Sushi pulled out her giant anchor and swung it around a few times for practice. Ana and Rebel looked at each other.

Without warning, Ana screamed. She and the puppy swam into the volcano, Ana with her sword drawn and Rebel with his teeth bared.

"For home," Edith and Wilber roared, shooting their weapons into the volcano.

CHAPTER 17

UNTIED ONIONS

Ana charged forward, and Rebel swam beside her, growling. Both Wilber and Edith unleashed laser fire and ice spells. When Ana got close, she swung her sword, smacking the orc in the helmet.

The orc recoiled.

"Waaaa?" he asked, stabilizing himself after the hit. He pulled out a giant harpoon and pointed at Ana. The gun fired, and a colossal spear was launched at the baby girl. Wilber aimed his rifle at the spear, pulled the trigger, and shot the harpoon. The metal sparked underwater, knocking it off course, so it completely missed Ana.

Sushi swam and hit the orc in the back with her anchor. All the merfolk cheered from their cages.

Edith sent an ice spell, freezing the orc's harpoon and breaking it. This opened Wilber up for a few more shots, hitting the orc in the stomach. Ana swung again; this time, the blade sliced open the orc's suit.

The orc screamed.

Edith shot an icicle at the tear in the orc's suit. It entered and expanded, causing the ugly guy to explode. Ice cubes shot everywhere, leaving only a couple of bones, some gold coins, and a key where the orc had been.

"Too easy," Wilber said, doing a dance he had learned from a videogame—or he tried the best he could without legs.

Cupcake swam in once the fight was over. He gathered all the loot and tossed the key to Sushi. "Free your people," he said.

Sushi smiled. She took the key and swam to all her friends. As fast as she could, she began unlocking the cages.

"Edith, how much time is left?" Wilber asked.

She looked uneasy. "We only have 20 minutes before we turn back into humans," she informed everyone.

As fast as they could, the children swam to the computers. Wilber was the best at video games, so he took the controls.

Once all the merfolk were free, Sushi swam down to the children. "How's it going?" she asked.

Wilber was too distracted to talk.

"Since he's not kicking or throwing things, he must be doing good," Edith guessed.

"Alright," Sushi nodded. "I'm going to take them to the armory. We're going to need all the help we can get."

"What do you mean?" Edith asked. "I thought we won."

Sushi shook her head. "All of Great Babylon is about to come crashing down on us. The fight hasn't even started."

"Oh great," Edith said. "And we only have a few minutes before we turn back into humans."

Sushi pulled out her coral controller. "Once you get what you want, I'll have the shell come straight to us."

Everyone nodded except for Wilber. He was clicking buttons and swiping screens so fast that no one could keep up. "I almost have it," he said as Sushi swam away with her people.

Ana clapped.

"Wait a second," Wilber said, freezing in place. "I fink someone's making a call right now."

The screen showed two black squares. Under each square was text showing the location. One read Earth, and the other read Mermoni. They could hear people talking, but their voices were distorted.

Wilber pushed a few buttons, and the distorted voices translated into something they could understand.

"We can help prepare for your arrival," said a voice from Earth, "but even with our help, many will fight back."

"It won't matter," said the voice from somewhere else on Mermoni. "I'm about to lead an invasion force against one of our greatest enemies. Once that's done, there will be plenty of ships to send your way."

Edith's eyes grew wide. "Who's talking?"

Above the two black squares, a small blue button read, "Join Call."

"Should I push it?" Wilber asked.

"No!" Cupcake shouted. "They'll see your face and know who you are. Let's just wait. Maybe they'll say their names. It'll be safer."

"But we have to hurry," Edith warned. "We only

have a few minutes before we turn back into humans. And who knows what army will show up here to stop us."

Sushi swam up. "My people joined the fight outside, but it's not going well. The monsters are almost here."

"Ahh," Wilber screamed, pushing the button.

A third square appeared, showing the computer's view of Sushi, Cupcake, and the children. Also, the two black boxes opened, revealing Razorface on Mermoni and dozens of people from Earth. Each human sat at a table with their country's name and flag on the front.

"I thought you said Razorface was a good guy?" Wilber asked.

"He's the best," Cupcake said, feeling defensive.

Sushi growled in anger. "Or, at least, we thought he was."

The building's name was written on the wall behind all the humans. Wilber struggled to read the words. "Where is the... Untied Onions?"

"It says 'United Nations,'" Edith groaned. "Wherever that is, and whoever they are, they're trying to give Earth to Babylon."

Everyone in the United Nations looked nervous. "Fix this," one of them said. Their camera quickly turned off, leaving only the children and Razorface.

"You know I have to kill you now, right?" the orc asked.

"I looked up to you," Cupcake shouted. "How could you be with Babylon?"

At the opening of the volcano, hundreds of undead sea creatures appeared. They flooded through the hole like water from a faucet.

"Run!" Sushi ordered.

Everyone left the magma pit and swam to one of the caves. Both Wilber and Edith fired their weapons behind them as monsters rained down.

Edith shot a spell at a giant ghost whale, but the icicle went right through and hit a mummy fish. "We're out of time," she warned. It was already getting harder to breathe underwater.

Ana swung her sword at a were-walrus in front of them. It howled as the blade knocked off a tusk.

"Our scales are falling off," Wilber said, swimming as hard as he could. "We're turning human again."

Sushi grabbed her coral controller and spoke loudly. "Ship, come to me," she said before turning back to the children. "It'll park at the exit. Just don't drown before you get there."

The kids continued to kill undead creatures, and as they exploded into loot, Cupcake gathered the prizes. But the killing was getting harder, and so was the swimming. At the end of the tunnel, they could see the light from Sushi's ship.

"I can't breathe," Edith said, but only bubbles came out of her mouth. No sound.

Ana stopped moving, and her eyes were closed.

"I don't think they're going to make it," Sushi said, grabbing the two girls. She swam as fast as she could, pulling the children with her.

Wilber was also human again. He leaned back and pointed his gun down the tunnel. He held the trigger, and the blasts from his rifle propelled him to the exit. Wilber flew into the shell first. Sushi and the girls were next. Cupcake and Rebel got in last.

As soon as they were inside, the door shut, and water drained from the shell. They all gasped for air as soon as they could get their head above water.

"That... was... close," Wilber said, struggling to talk.

Edith was also gasping. "But we... made it," she said, smiling.

Sushi turned back into a human, snarling as she grabbed control of the ship. "Not yet; we haven't." Sushi said. "We have to get out of here before they destroy my ship."

CHAPTER

THE BACK GATE

The space shell flew straight up. Spooky monsters swam after them, but the light scared them away as they got closer to the surface. A geyser of water exploded upward as the ship flew into space.

"We did it!" Edith said.

The children held hands and danced around in a circle, celebrating. Rebel barked happily around them.

They celebrated for a bit longer, but the children noticed their excitement was not shared. A sad feeling surrounded them. Laughter no longer felt appropriate.

Sushi sat at the controls and piloted with a blank

expression on her face. Cupcake slumped on a wooden bench. Even though there were no tears, he wiped his cheekbones, a reflex from when he was still human.

Their underwater adventure left their clothes soaked and their skin salty. Edith tried to wring out her hair as she walked to Cupcake, but the dampness of the shell made that impossible. "What's wrong?" she asked her friend.

Cupcake put his head in his hands. "I can't believe Razorface is bad."

Edith sat beside Cupcake and put her hand over his shoulder. "It'll be okay," she said, patting Cupcake on the back.

"It's not so bad," Wilber said, sitting down on the other side. "Bad guys always pretend to be good guys. It's in every show."

Cupcake grew uncharacteristically angry. He shot up, knocking away Edith's hand. "If Razorface can be bad, then anyone can!" he snapped. The outburst made everyone jump. Even he was startled by his own anger.

The room grew silent. One of the machines in the back clanked randomly, pushing bubbles into the ship. They popped and filled the room with oxygen.

Sushi shook her head. "I should have never trusted

an orc in the first place," she mumbled.

Ana waddled across the shell and pointed at the wall. "Uh-oh," she said.

Edith walked across the shell and knelt down beside her. "Do you need your diaper changed?"

"No! No!" Ana said, pushing her sister's face away with the palm of her chubby hand.

Edith frowned. "Well, what do you want, then?"

Ana waddled on her little baby legs closer to the wall. She pointed to a map of Uncle Ned, turned to the group, and said, "Azer fay."

Everyone exchanged confused glances.

Finally, a spark of recognition flashed in Sushi's eyes. "They're going after Ned."

Ana nodded. "Duh."

Edith stood up quickly. "Wait, what?"

"On the call, Razorface said he was going after one of Babylon's greatest enemies," Sushi explained. "He's going to attack Uncle Ned."

Again, everyone looked at each other.

Cupcake sat back down and slumped farther into his chair. "They won't even know what hit them. They think Razorface is good. They'll let him right in. And with a whole army of Babylon behind him"

"We have to warn them," Edith said. "Can we use your orb?"

Cupcake shook his head. "We're too far away."

Wilber held up his hand, flashing the ring. "Can't we use these?"

Cupcake turned his back to the group. His shoulders heaved as he tried to breathe. He was on the verge of sobbing. "Rings can't transport ships," he said, sniffling through the place where his nose should be. "And portals are almost impossible to find in space."

Wilber waved his hands around wildly. "We have to do something!"

Sushi walked over to the main controls. "We can use the Gate," she sighed.

Edith's eyes opened wide. "What's that?"

Cupcake pointed to the map on the wall. "There's a black hole on Uncle Ned. He drags it behind him with his back legs."

"What does a black hole do?" Edith asked.

Cupcake now looked to the group with a little bit of hope. "Ships can travel instantly between gates, and black holes can be used as gates."

"Wait. There's a black hole on Ned?!" Wilber exclaimed.

"Yeah, on his backside."

Wilber and Ana looked at each other. Both burst out laughing.

Cupcake stepped back. "What's so funny?"

The two giggled. "There's a black hole... on Uncle Ned's backside?!" Wilber said, struggling to hold back laughter.

Edith rolled her eyes.

"I don't get it," Cupcake said, puzzled and annoyed.

"It's not appropriate," Edith explained.

Everyone rolled their eyes except for Wilber and Ana. Both were now laughing hysterically.

"That's disgusting," Cupcake said.

"They're always like this," Edith explained before turning to Wilber. Her hands were on her hips, and her head was cocked to the side.

"Okay, okay," Wilber said. Once he finally stopped laughing, he took a deep breath. "So, can't we just find a black hole, use it, and warn everyone?"

Cupcake shook his head. "You need special permission to use it, and I bet Razorface has special permission," he groaned. "I bet he's taking an army through right now."

"There's no other way?" Edith asked.

"I know a guy from the Pirates Guild who could help us, but it'll be expensive," Sushi informed them. "I'll send him a message now."

"How much will it cost?" Wilber asked.

Sushi waited for a response, and when it came, she snarled in disgust. "It will cost us everything we just won from Mermoni," she said, shaking her head.

Cupcake reached into his apron. He pulled out a fist full of gold coins, microchips, and magical items. "We could almost buy a castle with all this," he explained. "Maybe even our own little planet. Are we sure we want to do this?"

Edith didn't let a second go by. "We have to do it," she said. "We can't just let people die."

Slowly, one by one, everyone nodded in agreement—everyone except for Rebel. The puppy instead gnawed furiously on Cupcake's left leg.

"Alright," Sushi said, plotting a course for the nearest warp point.

Sometime later, they arrived at a black hole.

"There it is," Sushi said.

From one angle, it looked like a tiny moon. As they approached, its odd form changed, swirling as violently as a hurricane. The children said a little prayer as Sushi piloted the ship forward. As they approached, they were pulled down into the swirling darkness.

"Hold tight. Flying through a gate messes with people," Sushi warned. "I once saw a guy poop his pants; he was so scared."

"Great," Wilber said, who had nearly pooped his pants on multiple occasions. "Do we have any wet wipes? Just in case?"

No one answered, and the shell flew closer to the gate. The force pushed against them before pulling them forward. It was like the top of a roller coaster, moments before the drop. It was like a slide so tall you couldn't see the bottom. It was like being on the merry-go-round at full speed.

Edith held her breath, and Ana whined loudly. Wilber tensed every muscle in his body and prayed he wouldn't poop his pants.

Seconds later, they tore through space like a rock through a wet paper towel.

The darkness faded, and they rose in the artificial light of Uncle Ned.

"Woah," Wilber said. He wobbled on his feet and held his stomach with both hands. "It felt like I was flushed down the toilet."

"Gross," Edith said.

Cupcake looked outside. "Did it work? Did we beat Razorface?"

A small harbor town lined the back of Uncle Ned's shell. There was the giant black hole where the water would be, surrounded by docks. Freighters and barges lined the dock while people loaded and unloaded their items: food, clothing, adventure gear, livestock, treasure, merchandise, etc.

Edith smiled. "We beat them here. No one looks scared or anything."

Cupcake smiled. "Now what?"

"Can we turn off the gate?" Edith asked.

"*We* can't, but they can," Cupcake explained, pointing to a building. It was next to the black hole and rose above the horizon like an airport control tower. "That place can open and close the Gate."

Wilber stood beside the mermaid. "Sushi, can you get us there?"

Sushi nodded, flying over to the control tower. The shell hovered above a small balcony. She opened the door, and everyone but her jumped out. "I'm out of ammo, but I'll see if I can get some of the other ships prepared to fight," she said, shouting from the ship. "But that'll only slow them down."

The children nodded. They turned around and entered the tower through a glass door with a sign that said, "Authorized Personnel Only." Inside was a room filled with many creatures. They all seemed shocked to see the children.

An airplane stood up. He had eyes where the windows should be and a mouth under his propeller nose. "Who are you?" he asked with a voice that sounded like wind.

"Babylon is about to come through the gate," Edith warned. "You have to shut it down."

Everyone in the control tower laughed.

"Little girl, stop wasting our time," the plane said. He pointed to the giant sword far off in the distance. "Great Babylon hasn't attacked Uncle Ned since Wackadoo stabbed him with that."

Wilber held up his fists, ready to swing at the airplane. "Lock it down," he threatened.

Before anyone could respond, a robotic voice announced, "Razorface is requesting gate access. Would you like to open the gate now?"

"Don't do it!" Wilber yelled. "He's actually Babylon."

Everyone in the tower rolled their eyes or laughed. "Yeah, right, kid," the plane said, pressing a button. "Permission granted."

"No!" the children shouted.

The whole island shook as a giant paw emerged from the portal.

The fingers were as large as lighthouses, and the arm was the size of a skyscraper. While the limb was through the gate, it wasn't completely stable. The furry skin was pixelated, hollow, and ghostly. Still, the paw swatted at a blimp. The colossal balloon was punched out of the air like a tiny bug. It exploded instantly. Clouds of fire and wreckage fell to the docks, catching other ships on fire and destroying buildings.

Wilber's jaw dropped. He slowly turned to the living airplane. "Good going, poopoo head."

"Wilber!" Edith shouted. "It's not his fault. Razorface had everyone fooled."

Her brother nodded reluctantly.

Edith then turned to one of the other people in the tower. It was a half-bird and half-fish creature. She looked it in the eyes and spoke in a calm voice. "Is there a way to send it back?"

"Uh," the creature stammered. "The arm hasn't fully

materialized yet. So... uh... if we can shut the gate, the arm will... uh... get pulled back to ... um... wherever it came from."

"Then do it!" the children said in unison.

"But that takes time," the living plane explained.

Wilber took a step forward. "The longer it takes, the more people die. How can we make it go faster?"

The half-bird-fish creature spoke up. "If you attack him... um... well, that'll slow his entry. And... uh... That might make it easier... to close the gate."

Ana clenched both fists. She tilted her head back and yelled to the sky. "War!" she screamed. Sensing her desire for battle, Rebel ran and laid beside her. She pulled herself onto his saddle and led her siblings out the door.

CHAPTER 19
GIANT RED EYES

"Wait for us," Edith begged, following her sister to the balcony.

Ana pulled on the reins, and the puppy skidded to a stop.

"Now what?" Wilber asked.

They surveyed the scene. The arm destroyed ships and buildings as it reached from the black hole. All over the port, hundreds of creatures cried out in fear. "Run away," they said. "We're all going to die." They were trampling one another, trying to get to safety.

"He's too powerful," Wilber told his sisters.

"Look," Edith said, pointing to a speaker. Hanging from the side of it was a little hand-held radio. "Should we call for help?"

Wilber picked up the communicator. He held down the button to test it. "Stinky booger breath," he said. His words echoed across the entire port. Hundreds of speakers were everywhere, and some even translated his words into other languages.

"It's not for making calls; it's for making announcements," he explained. "What should I say?"

"Let me see it," Edith asked, holding out her hand. Wilber passed it over.

"Everyone, listen to me!" she shouted. "We can stop the titan, but we have to do it together."

Not a single person stopped running, but a few slowed down to listen.

"We can weaken the arm and push him back," Edith explained. "Show them."

Wilber aimed. He had never attempted a shot from so far. Taking a deep breath, he opened fire. Lasers peppered the skin, causing a ripple of pixels across the arm. When the waves faded, the solid places were more translucent than before.

Edith leaned against the railing, so she could be

seen by everyone in the port. "See?" she exclaimed. "We can do this."

Wilber leaned over and spoke into the communicator. "But it will take all of us."

A few people stopped running, but most did not. Others hid behind barrels, in shops, and under docks. Some quarreled among themselves, fighting to board ships.

"They aren't listening," Edith told her siblings.

Cupcake pointed to the black hole. "Oh no," he said, his boney teeth chattering.

An army of orcs crawled from the portal.

With torches, they set fire to the buildings, while others chased the slower citizens of Ned. But faster than the fire, fear spread through the docks. The orcs were like a dark stain stretched across the once bright and cheery dock.

That's when the titan made his move. The head of a giant red panda pulled through the gate. There was a red glow in the eyes, and rabid white foam poured from its mouth.

"It's Wackadoo," someone yelled.

"He's come to finish Ned," screamed another.

The already messy scene now turned chaotic. At

this rate, the port would soon be completely taken over by orcs.

Wilber pulled the speaker from Edith's hand. He held down the button and shouted into it. "Fine, you big babies. We'll do this ourselves." He threw the communicator down and crawled onto the railing. Using his wing boots, he leaped off the tower. As he jumped across the port, he fired his weapon continuously at the arm.

"Me!" Ana yelled, directing Rebel to jump off after him. She waved her sword around like a crazy person, and as the puppy used his dash belt, she sliced an orc in half. He exploded into a cloud of bones and gold coins. Rebel howled happily, bouncing Ana from alley to alley. As they went, Ana cut orc after orc in half.

Meanwhile, Edith shot ice blasts at the titan. The more she shot, the larger they got. "Stop hurting people," she screamed loudly.

"Ned," Wackadoo roared. "I'm going to finish what I started."

Sushi was also in the fight. Even though the space shell had run out of ammo and bombs, she found other ways to help. By flying close to the arm, she distracted the titan. This allowed the other ships to escape.

Cupcake moved through the port, making brownies, potions, and bandaids. People were being hurt everywhere, and he tried to heal them all.

While the squad struggled to do significant damage, their bravery was making an impact—not on the titan—but in the hearts of those around them. Every person they saved, protected, or healed became another fighter that joined the battle.

People everywhere were pulling out weapons and giving their all to the fight. On docks and buildings, weapons unleashed a storm of damage against the giant red panda. Magic, missiles, and lasers all exploded on the arm.

Now Sushi was leading other ships against the Titan. She took the lead position between a group of WWII fighter planes. Once they completed their bombing run, a chubby-looking dragon flew in. She dropped an egg on Wackadoo's face, and rotten yolk exploded in his eyes.

"You can't stop this," the titan shouted, wiping away shells and goo. "Babylon always wins." Its massive body pulled and stretched towards the sword lodged in Uncle Ned's back. Even though not fully downloaded from the gate, the titan eclipsed the artificial sun that orbited the giant crab.

As the shadow cast darkness across the port, people shouted in fear. The only light came from the burning buildings, a few weapons, and Wakadoo's red eyes.

Edith stopped shooting spells. She could sense everyone's desire to run away and picked up the radio again. "Don't be afraid," she shouted. "We can win, but only if we fight together."

Throughout the whole battle, Uncle Ned had been running through space. He reached a small cluster of asteroids and jumped for them. As he flew, he twisted his body so that a small planetoid would graze over his back. As it did, it collided with Wakadoo, hitting him right in the face. Rocks the size of houses exploded from a cloud of dust that circled the giant red panda.

With that, even the most fearful citizens joined the fight. More bullets, spells, and cannons fired upon the titan, making it almost entirely pixelated.

A woman's voice came over the speaker. "The gate will close in 30 seconds. 30-29-28," she said, counting down.

"Come on, everyone," Wilber shouted to a group of bumblebees the size of cats. "Just a little longer." A swarm of them rocketed from his location, stinging the furry arm. As they did, Wackadoo screamed out in pain.

Every attack pushed the titan deeper into the gate. At 15 seconds, his head was sucked back in. At 7, it was just his hand. And when the countdown hit 0, the titan had disappeared entirely.

"The gate is closed," the robotic voice echoed over the speaker. "No incoming or outbound travelers will be permitted at this time."

"We did it," Edith said over the intercom, and everyone cheered. At the same time, the magic confetti fell from above. Trumpets blasted from nowhere, and fanfare echoed all around them. All across the port, as XP was gained, numbers appeared over the heads of a hundred people. An epic choir of voices chanted otherworldly lyrics, and a heroic voice said, "Level up."

Wilber used his wing boots to jump back onto the tower. Rebel also dashed up there, taking Ana with him. The written number "2" appeared over each of their heads.

"We leveled up!" Wilber cheered, feeling slightly stronger.

But the celebration did not last long.

Five soldiers grabbed the children by the arm and

put a muzzle on Rebel. The puppy whimpered as they lifted him off the ground.

"You are coming with us," said one of the soldiers.

Wilber tried to pull his arm away. "What are you doing?" he asked. "We just saved the day."

"The council has called an emergency session, and your presence is required."

Edith also tried to pull away but couldn't. "You don't have to be so mean about it," she said.

The soldier strengthened his hold around her arm, and she cried out in pain.

"Your presence is not optional," he said, throwing Edith into a cage. Sushi and Cupcake were already inside. Eventually, they threw in Wilber, Ana, and Rebel.

A giant eagle swooped in and carried the cage to the capital.

CHAPTER

20

MIDDLE OF A WAR

"Why'd they arrest us? Where are they taking us?" Edith asked. In her mind, she pictured herself cold and alone in prison.

"We saved *everything*," Wilber said to the eagle transporting them. "This isn't fair."

Sushi folded her arms and leaned back, unphased.

Cupcake wrung his hands. The bones made a clicking sound as they ground against each other. "This is bad," he mumbled to himself. "This is *so* bad."

The eagle flew for what seemed like hours. The bird's giant wings slowed when they finally got to the capital. Without warning, the cage dropped into a hole on the capital building. It landed with a thud, and everyone inside fell to the ground.

"So sorry about this," a bunny said, opening the cage doors. He stood on two legs like a human but had extra-long rabbit ears. "Everything is in chaos, and this was the fastest way we could bring you here."

"But we won," Wilber corrected him. "How can there be cay-ots."

"The implications of what just happened have everyone a little tense. The senators are trying to figure out how to respond," the bunny explained, shifting his shoulders uneasily. "Follow me."

The squad followed the rabbit to a waiting room at the end of the hallway.

"Fancy," Edith said. Everything in the room was made of marble. Gold trim and artwork lined the walls.

"The leaders called an emergency meeting. Once they reach a conclusion, a representative will be in," the rabbit explained. "Until then, please help yourself to some snacks."

Along the wall was a long table with a silky white cloth. Silver platters filled the top, displaying piles of candy, cake, beef jerky, and every kind of potato chip. Also, there was a pop machine with over 30 different flavors.

"So cool," Wilber said, shoveling a handful of sugary cereal into his mouth.

Ana and Rebel ran to the pop machine. She and the puppy stood underneath, allowing the soda to fall directly into their mouths. "Sticky," Ana giggled as soda showered them and spilled onto the floor.

Edith walked to the window. "This is making me nervous," she said.

Cupcake stood beside her. "Me too. I've never seen so much commotion."

Sushi examined the room, feeling along the walls, pulling out drawers, and looking behind picture frames. "Why'd they take our weapons?" she asked.

About an hour passed before the bunny returned. Edith had just finished cleaning all the soda off Ana and was now pulling chunks of candy from Rebel's fur.

"Please take a seat," the bunny said. "Senator Purdie is on his way."

"Woah," Cupcake said, astonished. "I don't know anyone who's ever met a Senator in real life."

Even Sushi seemed impressed.

A tall and handsome man entered the room. He had beautiful white angel wings, and he wore an expensive-looking suit.

"I hope you'll accept my apologies," Purdie said, flashing a charming smile. "What an exciting day."

"I voted for you," Cupcake blurted out.

Senator Purdie put his hand over his heart affectionately. "Thank you, that means so much."

"Are we in trouble?" Edith asked.

"Heavens, no," Purdie said. "Well, no more so than any of us."

"What does that mean?" Edith asked.

"It means that I've failed as a leader," he admitted. His tone was dignified and yet sincere. "Generations of safety... then today, on my watch, Ned almost fell to Babylon. And at the hands of Wackadoo, no less."

"Yeah," Wilber agreed, nodding his head. "That's pretty bad."

"Well, luckily, we had Edith, Wilber, Ana, Rebel, Sushi, and Cupcake," Purdie said with a warm smile. "You uncovered a pretty dangerous plot. But I have to admit, I already had suspicions about Razorface. That's why I had Desh join his squad."

The ninja suddenly appeared in the corner of the room.

Wilber's eyes opened wide. "Have you been in here

the whole time!" he shouted. "You're super sneaky."

"Follow me," Purdie said. He got up, and everyone walked behind him. "From what I understand, you're trying to protect your homeworld. Is that correct?"

Ana nodded. "Mama," she said a little louder than appropriate.

"Well, I may be able to help," Purdie said. "That is if you're willing to help me."

The children looked at each other. Wilber shrugged.

"What do you want us to do?" Edith asked.

"Over the next few days, there will be a full investigation. That's why I had you rushed here. We don't know how many people on Ned were with Razorface, and they might try to get revenge on you," Purdie warned. "But no matter what our investigation finds, we know Ned is safer now, thanks to you."

"No problem," Wilber said. He held up his hand for a high five, but no one gave it to him.

Purdie led everyone to an elevator, and they rode it down. "I don't know if you were just lucky or have a knack for mystery, but either way, I'd like your help tracking down other spies from Babylon."

"That seems like a big job," Edith said. "We're only at Level 2."

Purdie nodded. "Desh would join your squad and be my eyes and ears," he explained. "In return, I'd use my resources to protect your home. I help you; you help Uncle Ned."

The elevator door opened to a parking garage. There was a long car parked in front of them. The top was down, and all the seats were empty. The car was alive and honked to say, "Hello."

"Seems fair to me," Wilber said.

"I appreciate your enthusiasm, but your decision has to be unanimous," Purdie told the squad. "The missions ahead will be as hard as anything you've faced so far, if not worse."

Edith smiled confidently. "God has brought us this far. He'll keep protecting us."

"Excellent," Purdie said.

"But what about you?" Edith asked Desh. "You don't know us very well. Would you want to join us?"

The ninja didn't say anything at first. His face covering made it hard to tell, but he looked puzzled. "No one's ever asked me what I've wanted before," he said. "But I'll do anything to help Senator Purdie."

"It's settled then," the angel said. "Now, if you could get into this car. Everyone's waiting."

"Uhhh," Wilber said, confused. "Who is?"

A garage door opened in front of them. Along both sides of the road, there were thousands of people. They were cheering, lighting fireworks, and throwing flowers into the street.

"Your fans," Angel said with a smile. "You saved the island, and everyone wants to say thanks."

The children got into the car, and it pulled out of the building. As they drove through the streets of Ned, they thanked God. They had found the spies on earth, made new friends, and helped people who needed it. And while it had been more challenging than they expected, it brought them closer together as a family.

Still, as the people of Uncle Ned showered them with praise, the children felt afraid. There were powerful people back home who wanted Earth destroyed. Also, Razorface knew the children had stopped his plan. They were now in the middle of a war that raged across a million worlds, and they felt God calling them deeper into it.

While much of their future was shrouded in doubt, one thing was for sure: extraordinary days lay ahead.

Made in the USA
Coppell, TX
06 October 2022

84171414R10108